Ace and Christi Series

MIRACLE AT CAMP FRIENDSHIP

by

Sarah Hopewell

Illustrated by
John Truman

SCHOOL OF TOMORROW®

Lewisville, Texas

SCHOOL OF TOMORROW
P.O. Box 299000
Lewisville, Texas 75029-9000

©2000 Accelerated Christian Education,® Inc.

ISBN 1-56265-066-1
1 2 3 4 5 Printing/Year 04 03 02 01 00
Printed in the United States of America

TABLE OF CONTENTS

CHAPTER 1

ADVENTURE AHEAD

"Good night, Pudge. I'm so thankful you are home safe and sound." Mom kissed me on the cheek and closed the door.

Safe and sound. Now there were three words that meant more than they ever had before.

Let me explain. Most of the time nothing exciting ever happens to me—Pudge Meekway. For those of you I haven't met before, I'm just your ordinary, freckle-faced eleven-year-old. But when Mom said "safe and sound," it made me thankful all over again that I know God in a personal way. I've always thought I was glad to be on His side. I had no idea how much it would mean to have Him on my side. I know better now and have found He is the best friend of all.

I just had a nice **hot** shower and the best bedtime snack ever. I want to crawl under my nice warm covers and sleep like a caterpillar in his cocoon, but I can't until I explain those wet, muddy clothes hanging out of my clothes hamper. Then you will understand what "safe and sound" really means to me tonight.

You see, less than thirty-six hours ago, a group of us packed up, climbed aboard our Highland Church bus, and headed for the mountains for a weekend retreat at Camp Friendship. What a time we had, and what blessings we experienced!

My closest friends went on the retreat. You may know them. There is Ace Virtueson, of course. I suppose you could say he is sort of our leader and always seems to know what's right in every situation. The best athlete among us is Racer Loyalton. He looks something like me, except he's thinner. Booker Thriftmore is also athletic, and I was glad he and his father went along. His dad owns a repair business in Harmony. Mr. Thriftmore's hammer and saw came in very handy during the retreat. Hapford Humblen went too. He is the quiet type, but his simple wisdom is often something with which you can't argue. J. Michael Kindhart and Reginald Upright have the brains. It's always a challenge keeping up with them. You wouldn't believe the big words they sometimes use.

Christi Lovejoy, Miriam Peace, and Sandy McMercy also went along. They are my friends too, but since they are girls, I don't spend as much time with them as I do with the boys.

Then there are Ronny Vain and Susie Selfwill. They live a few blocks from Highland Church. I will tell you more about them later. For now, I'll just say that they help us build our Christian character.

The bus trip to Camp Friendship was to take about two hours, so Pastor Alltruth felt that those of us going should pack up and leave as soon after noon on Friday as possible.

Oh, I almost forgot to tell you who our adult sponsors were. I hadn't expected Pastor Gentle from Harmony to go, but it turned out to be a special treat to have him along. Pastor Gentle loves boys and girls, and he lives up to his name. He never has an unkind word for anyone. He is so wise and understanding—you know, the grandfatherly type who always has a "word to the wise" for every situation. You can't help but like him.

Mr. Friendson, my Learning Center supervisor, was in charge of the retreat, and he ran things by the clock—I mean that literally. What a guy! I saw a new side of him, for sure. He has more energy than any of us boys, and I think he saved up some extra for the retreat. He also knows how to drive a bus, so he was our bus driver for the trip.

Miss Content, who teaches the young children how to read, went to oversee the girls' lodge. Yes, a "lodge" is what Mr. Friendson called where we stayed. It sounds like a resort, doesn't it? . . . but more about our "lodge" later.

In order to go on the retreat, everyone had to have a permission slip signed by a parent. The slip clearly stated that we needed a sleeping bag, and we were each allowed a backpack and one overnight bag. It did not say how big a bag, however. Since we were going to be "roughing it," it was recommended we each bring a flashlight and any other small camping items that might be useful.

Hapford Humblen, with his big heart, had gotten permission to invite Ronny Vain to come along. I didn't think it was a good idea, and I told him so.

"Hapford, you know that Ronny is constantly teasing you and trying to get you into trouble. Why do you want to invite him when it might spoil your whole weekend?" I warned.

"'What better way to get rid of an enemy than to make a friend out of him?' That's what Mr. Friendson always says." Hapford had done it again. With his simple logic he had gotten my thinking back on track.

"You preach Mr. Friendson's sermons as well as he does, Hapford," I had to say sheepishly. For the rest of the weekend, I tried to remember that sermon.

The truth is, that's what Camp Friendship is all about—making friends.

In my mind, I could already envision Camp Friendship. I could see log lodges with curls of smoke floating up from their huge stone fireplaces into the brilliant blue fall sky. The trees would be alive with color—bright yellow and burnt orange and sienna. Mornings would be brisk and refreshing, and the air would be full of fall smells like hickory smoke, pine needles, and dry leaves. Then, after a restful night's sleep, the smell of country ham, gravy, hot biscuits, maple syrup, and eggs would welcome a new day.

I had never been to the mountains where Camp Friendship is located, but I had seen pictures. As Pastor Alltruth described them, the peaks and valleys were rugged but beautiful and especially breathtaking in the fall. He did recommend we take warm clothing since the camp was located at a high elevation.

Camp Friendship? Well, I had never been there either. In fact, I hadn't even seen pictures of it. All Pastor Alltruth said was that it would be an experience we would always remember. He even said it might change our lives, as it had the lives of

others. I didn't know how, but I felt certain the weekend retreat would leave us with many special memories, and it certainly did!

CHAPTER 2

GETTING ON THE ROAD

Friday morning I was so excited about the trip that I had a very hard time concentrating on my schoolwork. When lunchtime finally rolled around, I swallowed half my lunch without chewing it. (Mom is always reminding me not to do that.) Later, as we were loading the bus, I felt as if I had swallowed a rock instead of a roast beef sandwich.

The boys loaded their stuff first, since it took the girls longer to get changed into their casual clothes for the trip. When Ronny Vain showed up, all he had was his sleeping bag and a small backpack. His pack matched him perfectly. It was slim and trim. "I'll just throw it up here in the overhead rack," Ronny said, as he climbed aboard the bus to stake out his seat. Mr. Friendson and Mr. Thriftmore, who were doing the packing, seemed satisfied with that arrangement.

Ronny, with his black shock of hair bouncing, ran off, calling over his shoulder, "I'm going to find Hapford."

If I were to describe Ronny's personality, I suppose I would say he is likable but scrappy. In my mind, I predicted that having him along was likely to present some interesting situations.

Finally, Sandy McMercy and Christi Lovejoy showed up. "Mr. Friendson, where do you want our luggage?" asked Sandy. Her red bangs were damp with perspiration as she wrestled with the biggest duffel bag I have ever seen. Christi's was a little smaller, but it was bulging more. What were really bulging were Mr. Friendson's eyes.

"Girls, we're only going for the weekend. How could you possibly need so much for such a short trip?"

"It's just things." That was all Christi said, but her brown eyes danced with mystery as she and Sandy skipped away.

What could he say? The permission slip had stated one bag, and they each had only one bag.

"Don't worry, Mr. Friendson. My bag won't take up much room."

It was Miss Content. She had a tightly wrapped sleeping bag and only a small overnight case that fit easily under a seat. Mr. Friendson smiled approvingly.

When all the suitcases, gym bags, overnight cases, sleeping bags, and those two BIG duffel bags were finally loaded and everyone seemed to be aboard,

Mr. Friendson started the bus. Miss Content counted heads. Everyone was there and ready to go—except one.

"We really do need to get on the road," Pastor Gentle commented.

The holdup was Susie Selfwill. When she had heard about the retreat and that Ronny was going, she invited herself. Miss Content and the girls agreed it was a good opportunity to get to know her better, but now she was late. So what else was new?

"Go without her." That was Ronny's solution, and I half agreed. He reasoned, "She knew what time we were leaving. I was here on time. She should have been too." He had no sympathy, or patience for that matter. It would be nice if I could say it was the last time he showed that spirit.

Mr. Friendson hated to do it, but we were finally forced to leave without Susie. "We really can't wait any longer. The folks at the camp are expecting us," was the final conclusion. I believe Christi, Miriam, Sandy, and Miss Content were genuinely disappointed that Susie would not be going.

As hard as it was to get along with Susie, the girls cared about her. They wanted to be her friend. She did not have an easy home life. Her mother worked long hours at a nearby factory, and Susie was often on her own.

Our bus had just turned the corner at the end of the block when a whirlwind of dark hair, flapping sweatshirt sleeves, and sagging socks came flying toward us. It was Susie, and she was waving like a fluttering flag. Mr. Friendson pulled to the curb and opened the folding bus door.

She immediately began making excuses. "Why did you leave early? If I had had more time, I could have found my new gym bag! The zipper broke on this old one, and my clothes fell out all over the sidewalk! I almost lost my backpack too! I laid it down with my sleeping bag while I was picking up my clothes, and some stray dog tried to carry it off!"

Miss Content pushed her way to the front of the bus while the rest of us just sat there staring in amazement. Amazing! That word pretty well sums up Susie.

Quickly Miss Content broke our stunned silence. "Ah-ah-Susie, do you have your signed permission slip?"

"Right here!" Susie proudly whipped it out and handed it to Miss Content. She certainly was full of surprises. Next, she proceeded to jostle her way past several seats until she reached the one where Miriam was sitting. She plopped herself and her backpack down with a big sigh. Miss Content stood on the bus steps with Susie's sleeping bag and disheveled gym bag at her feet. She and Pastor Gentle looked at each other helplessly. What other challenges might Susie present before these two days were over?

CHAPTER 3

A, B, C, D, E, F, G, . . .

No more surprising things happened, and we were on our way to the mountains and Camp Friendship. It was going to be a long trip.

"Why did the luggage have to go in the back?" questioned Booker. "I was looking forward to sitting on one of the back seats. That's where the boys always sit. When the bus goes over big bumps, we bounce up and down as if we were on bungee cords. I figure the road up the mountain will have lots of bumps."

"Well, the idea was to balance the load better and **not** have the bus bouncing up and down so much," explained Mr. Thriftmore. "It might be fun for you, but it's not good for the bus or for the springs in the seats."

"Okay. I guess we'll have to find something else to do so the trip won't seem so long."

"I agree. 'An idle mind is the devil's workshop.'" It was Pastor Gentle in characteristic form. "Maybe I have some ideas."

Maybe? I believe he had appointed himself to see that we were not bored on the trip. Maybe he remembered how long two hours on a hard bus seat can be.

At any rate, we were soon merrily riding along. Mr. Friendson, baseball cap firmly planted on his head, was whistling some spirited tune, and Miss Content was twittering with the four girls. Miriam Peace, the only girl from Harmony to come on the retreat, was now getting better acquainted with Susie Selfwill. It was obvious Susie had claimed Miriam's company for the trip, and, as it turned out, for the whole weekend. Pastor Gentle and Mr. Thriftmore stationed themselves in the middle of the bus with us boys.

"Did you bring any special camping gear, J. Michael?" Ronny asked.

"I brought a flashlight," answered J. Michael. "It's a nice one too. My dad bought it special for me for this retreat."

"Talk about flashlights," Racer and I chimed in together, but Racer finished, "you should see the one Reginald brought. It has a regular flashlight on one end and a flasher on the other end." Reginald smiled modestly from the seat behind.

Mr. Thriftmore asked, "Did everyone bring a canteen? You will probably need one if we go on a long hike."

"A little fishing line and a few hooks are also useful," added Pastor Gentle before anyone could answer. From his pocket, he pulled out a little plastic box and rattled it.

It was then that Racer pulled out his Super Sport. Talk about gadgets! It had a can opener, knife, fork, spoon, file, screwdriver, and even a saw blade, among other things.

"Dad lent it to me for the weekend. He always carries it with him when he goes on surveying trips. With this, a person can survive in the woods for days," he boasted.

"You guys act like you're going to get stranded in the woods or be camping out for a week. All a person really needs is a compass," bragged Ronny. He was always crowing about something. "If you have one, you can't get lost—that is, if you know how to read it."

Then he pulled a closed fist out of his pocket and showed us a small pocket compass about twice as big as a silver dollar. It didn't look like anything special to me, but he was guarding it as if it were some special treasure.

"See?" he said. "I have a compass, and it's a good one. My dad gave it to me. He showed me how to read it too. I'll never get lost in the woods as long as I have it with me . . . and I'm always going to have it with me."

That compass was very important to Ronny. He came from a broken home, so he didn't see his father often. Naturally, a gift from him would be prized. I understood, since I had no father at home either. My dad passed away when I was just five, but I did know something Ronny didn't know—the promise of my Heavenly Father that He is "a father of the fatherless." I also knew I'd be with my earthly father again someday in Heaven.

Pastor Gentle decided it was time to change the subject. "Say, have you fellows ever played the Alphabet Game?"

Hapford piped up, "You mean the one where you find words on signs to match the letters of the alphabet?"

"Well, I was thinking of a little different version of that game. We'll call it the Retreat Alphabet Game. This is how it goes. I say, 'I went on a retreat, and I took an *air mattress*.' Now, the next person has to remember what I said and add one more thing for the next letter of the alphabet. Ace, you be the next one, and we'll go around."

My friend Ace had been pretty quiet until now. He had been to Camp Friendship once before with his father and grandfather. For some reason, he wasn't as excited as the rest of us. He perked up when we started to play the game, though.

"I went on a retreat, and I took an *air mattress* and a . . . a *blanket,*" he said with enthusiasm and a pleased smile.

"Very good," commented Mr. Thriftmore. He went next. "I went on a retreat, and I took an *air mattress, a blanket, and a canteen.*"

It wasn't as much fun as softball, but it wasn't as hard either, and it did make the time pass. By the time we reached "u," "v," "w," "x," "y," and "z," we'd gotten the girls' attention. They were trying to help us with all kinds of gestures, which weren't any help at all, really. Finally Hapford came up with *yo-yo,* and Reginald finished with *zax.*

"What in the world is a zax?" accused Ronny. "I think you just made that up."

"I don't mean to be objectionable," answered Reginald with total confidence. (That guy has quite a vocabulary, as you can see.) "I assert that it is a very suitable word." He reached into his pocket. "I just happen to have my pocket dictionary. Look it up for yourself."

I wondered if Ronny even knew how to use a dictionary. We all waited to see who was right—I don't know why; no one ever wins in an argument.

Ronny **did** know how to use a dictionary. "Aw, it's here, but why couldn't you have come up with something simple? Something like a—a—a *zinc ointment.* That would have worked, and zinc ointment could come in handy on a retreat."

Not bad, I thought. But as I said, no one wins in an argument, and the feelings I had had about Ronny were not very kind. How could I ever show him God's love if I didn't have a loving heart and attitude toward him?

With the game over, we sang a few choruses. Then we stopped to get out and stretch and have a little snack. Getting back into the bus, we definitely were more comfortable and felt like napping.

Forget that! We started up the mountain road that led to Camp Friendship—not straight up, mind you, but wi-i-nding up. I never have handled those around-and-around, up-and-down, winding roads very well. What bothered me even more, though, was how at certain spots the edge of the road just seemed to drop off into nowhere. The girls squealed at the dizzying view. I wanted to squeal too, but I couldn't

let on that I was a little nervous. I just moved to the other side of the bus—the side away from the drop-off. There were guard rails along the drop-off, but I still preferred not to look. Instead, I swallowed hard and concentrated on my side of the road—the side closer to the side of the mountain. There were signs, so I read them instead of looking on the other side and down into the valley, which was dropping farther and farther away.

Deer Crossing
Sharp Turn
Lookout Ahead

"Should we stop?" called Mr. Friendson from the front.

"No way!" squealed the girls.

"Yes," countered Reginald.

He was truly enjoying our "precipitous situation," as he called it. Hapford slid into the seat with me. I don't think he felt comfortable by the window either, but neither of us were about to show our squeamishness. *"What time I am afraid, I will trust in thee,"* I kept quoting to myself, and I read some more signs. Thankfully we did not stop.

No Littering
No Guard Rails—*NO GUARD RAILS!!!*
Watch for Falling Rocks

There were a few places where rocks and a part of the bank beside the road had been washed down. We had been having a lot of rain lately. I scarcely noticed the next sign.

Mud Slides

Finally, the landscape leveled out. Right away I saw a sign that said CAMP FRIENDSHIP, and it had an arrow pointing to the right. We had arrived at our resort . . . er . . . retreat.

CHAPTER 4

WELCOME TO CAMP FRIENDSHIP

Like a tower of building blocks toppling over, my vision of "resort" Camp Friendship crumbled in the dust as the bus screeched to a halt just a short distance off the main road in a clearing about the size of a baseball field. Tall pines and smaller trees and shrubs totally shut us in. Even the camp sign disappeared from view. In front and to the right of the graveled clearing, the trees had been cut down.

We could see just two buildings. First was a long, narrow building covered with black tar paper. A row of dirty glass windows lined two sides, and a big black chimney stuck up above the sloped roof. A weather-beaten pine shingle dangled from one hook over the door. In scrawled letters, it read **Dining Hall.** A big bell with a rope hanging from it hung beside the door.

A smaller building, also wrapped in black tar paper, was next to the Dining Hall. The shingle there was neatly lettered and proudly announced **Camp Office.** On a narrow porch, an older gentleman and lady, nodding sleepily, sat in two rockers. She had a

red shawl wrapped around her shoulders, and he had a camouflage hat pulled down to his ears. Those were their two distinguishing features. Both wore spectacles far down on their noses, and they squinted in our direction as we drove up. The gentleman raised his hand to acknowledge our arrival. Obviously they were expecting us.

"Who are they?" questioned Susie without a minute's hesitation. I suppose she thought the rest of us knew, but Mr. Friendson and Pastor Gentle were the only ones who know.

"That's Aunt Ruth and Uncle Jake," Mr. Friendson said. "They've run this camp for forty years or more. I came here years ago as a youngster. It was a little different then."

"My dad came to this camp too," interjected Ace. "This is where he dedicated his life to the Lord. He said he owes a lot to Aunt Ruth, Uncle Jake, and Camp Friendship."

"I agree," continued Mr. Friendson, "and one good turn deserves another. That's one reason we're here."

I didn't know exactly what that meant, but I was still in shock.

"Now," continued Mr. Friendson, "before you get off the bus and take your things to the lodges, I think we should choose 'buddies.' We are in the mountains, far away from town. Most of you are unfamiliar with the wild, and any mistake or accident could have serious consequences. The buddy system will help us keep track of each other."

"Miriam's my buddy," Susie piped up, and she grabbed her new friend somewhat roughly by the arm. Miriam got her balance back and smiled sweetly as usual. I've never seen Miriam be anything but sweet-tempered. Not all of us are so good-natured. That left Sandy and Christi to be the other set of girl buddies. I assumed Hapford and Ronny would be buddies, and probably Ace and Racer. I didn't know whom Reginald would pair up with, maybe J. Michael. They were both "intellectuals." It didn't turn out that way, though. Ace chose J. Michael. Booker and Racer did a high-five to indicate their intentions, and, believe it or not, Ronny announced that he wanted us to be buddies. Pastor Gentle looked at me and said, "Let patience have her perfect work?" Then he winked. I got the message. God still had some rough edges He had to polish in my character. That left Hapford and Reginald as buddies. How about that?

"Come on now," said Mr. Friendson. "Let's go meet Aunt Ruth and Uncle Jake."

Do you know what? They hadn't moved since we arrived. They just kept rocking. I saw them later in the Dining Hall kitchen. They had a little table there. The lines in their faces seemed to say something was troubling them, but I had no idea what. *Maybe it's just a natural part of growing older,* I thought.

Now, none of what I just described went unnoticed. From the cover of the nearby woods, an uninvited guest was watching curiously. Our arrival took him quite by surprise. He shrank back into the shadows. Instinct from years of wearisome survival said, "Stay hidden."

Back at the bus, it was time to unload. Since this was not a resort after all, and there were no bellhops, we all proceeded to claim our luggage as Mr. Thriftmore and Mr. Friendson set it out.

"Where are the lodges?" asked Booker, looking all around.

J. Michael had a question too. "We aren't going to have to sleep in tents, are we?"

"No, no," chuckled Mr. Friendson. He pointed off to the left in the direction of some huge pines.

"That's south," announced Ronny, proudly pulling his compass out of his pocket again. I was slightly impressed, since he was my buddy.

Beyond the pines was a narrow path, thick with layers of pine needles. "Just follow the path," said Mr. Friendson. "The lodges are at the top of the ridge. Boys to the right . . . girls to the left . . . just past the fork in the path. The little buildings you pass just before each lodge are the washrooms."

I thought I knew what he meant, but I didn't ask. In the next ten minutes, I found out I was right. The lodges had no bathrooms—not even cold running water. In comparison to the lodges, the washrooms were quite elegant, and they had cold **and** hot running water—sometimes.

"When Dad and I came up here last year, we helped build the washrooms," Ace announced. Light was beginning to dawn. Ace knew what the rest of us had not known, and, as Pastor Gentle would have said, "He kept his lip buttoned." Had we known more precisely what "roughing it" really meant, we might not have been looking forward to the retreat with so much excitement.

While we mustered our strength to carry not only our luggage but also the girls' luggage to the lodges, a shrill blast split the air. It sounded just like the whistle Mr. Friendson blew at school when break time was over. We all stopped dead in our tracks and turned toward it.

Mr. Friendson was grinning at us. "Good," he said with the whistle still between his teeth. "I wanted to see if it would work. Meet me back here in forty-five minutes. We have lots of work to do before the dinner bell. Oh, Miss Content . . . Mr. Thriftmore, don't forget about the wood."

They nodded. A change had taken place in Mr. Friendson. Suddenly he had turned into a drill sergeant. Was there a conspiracy going on here?

Since we all had our marching orders, Miss Content led the girls to "Queen Esther's Lodge," and Mr. Thriftmore led us to—get this— "David's Hideaway Lodge."

When Mr. Thriftmore turned the doorknob at David's Hideaway Lodge, the door squeaked open on rusty hinges. A musty, dusty smell wrinkled our noses as our eyes tried to adjust to the dingy interior. Mr. Thriftmore flipped the light switch. The one large, bare bulb hanging from the rafters gave one quick flash and then left us in dinginess. The only other light was coming through dusty windows, all but one of which were closed. More light seeped through a slatted opening at the peak of the roof. A potbellied stove sat in the center of the room; and rusty, metal, old-style bunks lined two walls. A thin mattress lay uninvitingly on each. In the corner were a beat-up broom and dustpan. Some rags hung beside them on a peg. "Some resort," said Ronny sarcastically. The rest of us were speechless.

"I'll go get a new light bulb so we can see in here," said Mr. Thriftmore. "While I'm gone, you boys carry out the mattresses and beat them a little to get rid of some of the dust. Unroll your sleeping bags and get your beds ready. I should be back by then."

That's what we did, and clouds of dust flew up until we were coughing and sneezing. We shook and beat those mattresses for all we were worth. We must have looked pretty silly. It's creepy to think about it now, but again we were being watched from behind some nearby trees. In our wildest dreams, we had no idea what was going on. We didn't find out until later. Actually, we had taken someone's bed and chased him out of his temporary shelter.

By the time Mr. Thriftmore got back, we had finished making our beds and were looking for window sills or other places to store our toothbrushes, combs, soap, and other necessary sleep-over items.

Mr. Thriftmore started looking around for something to stand on so he could replace the light bulb, but he continued giving instructions at the same time. "Put your suitcases and backpacks under the beds. Ace and J. Michael, please open the rest of those windows. That will let in a little more light and help get rid of the musty smell. Hapford and Reginald, it would be helpful if you would get the broom and dustpan and sweep up a bit."

"What about us, Mr. Thriftmore?" asked Ronny. This was something new and interesting. Ronny was asking for a job.

"Of course," nodded Mr. Thriftmore, pleasantly surprised. "You and Pudge may carry in firewood. Stack it there by the stove," he said, pointing to a woodbox. "I have a feeling it will get pretty chilly tonight, and we'll need plenty of wood. Booker and Racer, come with me. We need to find a stepladder to reach that bulb." Without missing a beat, he added, "No fooling around, please. Mr. Friendson gave us forty-five minutes, and we don't want to be late."

We all had our assignments and got right at them. With the windows open, there really was more light, and I suppose our eyes were adjusting to the dinginess also.

Suddenly Hapford said, "Look, Reginald. Birds are roosting on the rafters." We all looked at where Hapford was pointing.

"Oh, no!" gasped Reginald. "Those aren't birds. They are bats—*chiroptera noctivagans,* I believe. Don't disturb them."

But it was too late. Hapford had already taken a swipe at them with the broom. Two of them started swooping wildly around the room.

"They're going to get in my hair!" shouted Ronny, waving his arms above his head.

"No, they aren't," insisted Reginald. "They have sonar."

The bats soon found their roost again.

"What's going on?" Mr. Thriftmore, Booker, and Racer were back with a stepladder.

"We have bats in the rafters," Hapford said. "What are we going to do to get rid of them?"

"Hm-m-m, that is a problem," said Mr. Thriftmore, taking off his cap and scratching his head.

"See that rusty rod hanging from the opening up there?" pointed out Ace. "When it gets dark, the bats will fly out through the slats, and we can use the rod to close the slats so they can't get back in. That's what we did last summer. I guess someone left the slats open, and the bats got back in."

All this time, we were still being watched. Our spy had opened the slats to air out the lodge, and he was also the one who had opened the window.

"It is also strange that a window was left open," said Ace. "When I was here with Dad, we made sure all the windows were closed before we left. Dad said that was one of the camp rules—'When you check out of your lodge, make sure all the windows are closed.'"

At the time, there seemed to be no explanation except that someone had broken the camp rule. Whatever the reason for the open window and the open slats, we were glad Ace had had some previous camp experience. Camp Friendship was like a different world, and he was our fearless leader.

With the bat situation settled, Mr. Thriftmore set about the task of replacing the light bulb. The ladder he found was in pretty bad shape.

"Racer, may I borrow your Super Sport to tighten some of these bolts?"

"Yes, sir," answered Racer enthusiastically. He was glad to find a reason to get it out and show off its special features. At the moment, Ronny couldn't find any good reason to get out his compass.

Mr. Thriftmore did what he could for the ladder but still asked Booker and J. Michael to steady it while he climbed up to replace the light bulb. When he finished, the room became much brighter. It looked better, too, with the beds made up and the floor swept. We had already made an improvement.

As Mr. Thriftmore climbed down the ladder, he declared, "Mr. Friendson will be blowing that whistle any minute now. Reginald and Hapford, close the windows before we leave. We don't want mosquitoes when we come back."

No, we certainly do not, I thought.

"Pudge . . . Ronny, please grab another armload of wood."

"We'll help them," volunteered J. Michael and Ace. We headed for the woodpile. I picked up some kindling, but Ronny rolled over a big log.

"Snake!! Snake!!" he yelled and started jumping up and down.

The boys all backed away, and Mr. Thriftmore came running. "Oh, that is just a lizard, not a snake," he informed. "It won't hurt you. Look, it has skittered up that tree."

"Lizards keep other unwanted things away," said Ace calmly.

"Oh, great!" declared Ronny.

Another new revelation? I wondered.

"Things like what?" questioned J. Michael. Evidently he wasn't too fond of lizards either.

"Things like spiders," Ace answered. "Did you see any spiders in the lodge?"

Now that he mentioned it, we hadn't. We supposed he had learned that last summer too, but did that mean there might be lizards **inside** the lodge?

"Lizards didn't keep the bats away," observed Hapford.

"Au-augh!" exclaimed J. Michael, "lizards as well as bats!" He drew his hand across his forehead as if he were about to faint.

Although we hadn't seen any lizards in the lodge—probably because we had no lights—the girls in Queen Esther's Lodge had. I suppose we hadn't heard the commotion over there because we were too busy with our own problems. The same person who was watching us also saw what happened at Queen Esther's Lodge. He felt Miss Content handled the lizard situation very well. She had grown up in the mountains, so she simply picked up one of the creatures to show that they were harmless. Susie thought that was neat. She tried it too and decided they were wonderful "pets."

When she discovered they could change color, she was really excited. Before the day was over, she had two or three lizards hanging from her jacket pockets. Eventually she found they would even hang from her ears. Even though I'm a guy, I am not that desperate for a pet.

Christi and Sandy were not jealous. They had brought their own pets . . . well, I suppose you couldn't exactly call them pets, but something like that. You see, one thing that took up so much space in each duffel bag was a "special friend." Snuggles was a big, white, floppy-eared, stuffed bunny dressed in a calico dress, and Cuddles was a cuddle-sized, light-brown teddy bear with a big blue bow under its chin.

"I never go on any trip without Cuddles," declared Sandy.

"And Snuggles sleeps with me every night," said Christi. "She is lonely without me."

None of this made sense to me, but then, I'm not a girl. Miriam didn't have any special friend, but she had some big, fluffy slippers, and she would soon find out a certain creature would try to make them its home.

CHAPTER 5

WORK TO DO

While we were getting settled and transforming our accommodations at David's Hideaway, Mr. Friendson was preparing for some transforming of his own. Back at the Camp Office, all kinds of cleaning supplies, garbage bags, buckets, rakes, shovels, hammers, and other odds and ends greeted us. Aunt Ruth and Uncle Jake rocked and watched with interest. I could tell they were glad to see the camp come alive with activity. I even caught a hint of a smile on Aunt Ruth's face.

The sun was shining brightly but beginning to dip toward the west. All our work getting settled at the lodge had warmed us up, and I thought of taking off my jacket, but then the thought crossed my mind that something might crawl into it.

Mr. Friendson blew his whistle. That startled Uncle Jake, and he adjusted his hearing aid.

Someone started to snicker, but Pastor Gentle quickly raised an eyebrow. He didn't have to say it. We all knew. ". . . honour the face of the old man, and fear thy God."

Our observer watched with interest. His plans hadn't included an active group of young people.

"Okay," began Mr. Friendson, "maybe you haven't noticed, but Camp Friendship could use some sprucing up."

"That's an understatement," announced Ronny.

Mr. Friendson continued, "There are some big jobs needing to be done, but there are many little tasks that would help. We're here to have a good time and have some new experiences. Pastor Gentle and I have been friends of Uncle Jake and Aunt Ruth for many years. This camp for young people has been their life ministry, but they're getting up in years now and can't keep up the camp. Highland Church and Harmony Chapel have agreed to help keep the ministry alive. We can help by doing a few odd jobs around here this afternoon. What do you say? Should we help our friends?"

Booker stepped forward. He crossed his arms high on his chest and looked down his nose. In his most dignified voice, he said, "As my pastor would say, 'A friend in need is a friend indeed.'"

Pastor Gentle laughed right out loud. He rocked forward and back on his heels. His whole torso shook good-naturedly in amusement at Booker's imitation of him.

"Of course, we'll help," we all chimed in.

"All right then." Again Mr. Friendson resumed his drill sergeant manner. "Girls, here are buckets, rags, and window cleaner. You may start cleaning windows on the inside. Start with the Dining Hall; then do the Camp Office. You may also do the windows at the lodges, but please be sure all the windows are closed and locked when you are finished." For some reason Mr. Friendson seemed to be putting special emphasis on closing and locking windows.

Turning to us boys, he continued, "Boys, I need someone to pick up pine cones and tree branches that have fallen on the ground."

"Why don't we do that?" I said to Ronny. He agreed, and we got some heavy leaf bags for the pine cones. Mr. Friendson instructed us to pile all the tree branches in an open spot where they could be burned later.

Ace and J. Michael ended up helping Mr. Thriftmore repair the shingle over the Dining Hall door, as well as the office steps, and some broken windows and door locks. Only later did he mention that someone or something had gotten into the kitchen uninvited. Ace suggested that it might have been a bear. He said his dad remembered a bear had caused some problems around the camp once when he was a camper. I was glad I didn't know all that before Ronny and I volunteered to gather up pine cones. Mr. Thriftmore felt it was more likely the work of a mother raccoon.

Racer and Booker worked with Pastor Gentle to clean windows on the outside. They had to spray and knock down some wasps' nests, but most of the wasps had died because of the cold nights.

There is just something about working together and helping friends in need. It sure feels good!

All the while, Mr. Friendson circled around like a hawk to give help and direction where needed. The ominous whistle hung around his neck, ready for use at any time. He was careful about blowing it though. He didn't want to blast Uncle Jake's eardrums again.

While we all worked enthusiastically, the uninvited visitor in the shadow of the trees watched with growing interest. He could not help but notice the shabbiness and disrepair of the camp. It had certainly changed over the years since he had last seen it.

Since none of us were aware of the shadowy observer, we forged ahead with our voluntary chores. Ronny and I gathered fallen branches and pieces of wood and carried them to the pile. Some were so large and heavy it took both of us to drag them. At times Ronny appeared to be different in this "back-to-nature" setting. I thought it must be because he was away from the bad influences of the city. He still bragged a lot, but I thought being buddies must be helping him feel more accepted. After we finished with the branches, we each got a bag and began to fill it with pine cones. There were lots of them, and we wandered around picking them up.

"Look," I said softly. A squirrel was standing on his hind legs looking at us. When we moved, he ran. We dropped our bags and tried to follow him. He ran up a pine tree, skittered across a branch, and then leaped to the branches of a gigantic oak. We stood there watching him for a moment. His tail swished up and down rhythmically. He seemed to be listening.

"Maybe he's sending some kind of message," Ronny speculated as he took a step toward the tree. Mr. Squirrel raced down the trunk, and then scurried across the dry leaves and deeper into the forest. Finally he got so far ahead of us that we lost him, or maybe he was hiding among the branches. The sun had set, and it wasn't easy to see.

"We lost him," Ronny said disappointedly. He gave one last look around. Suddenly he jerked toward me and slapped my arm. "Pudge, where are our pine cones?"

I looked around. "I don't know. Where did we leave them?"

"Which way did we come? Where's the camp?"

My breath caught, and my face felt hot. I didn't know.

"We're lost. Help! We're lost. Somebody help us!" Ronny panicked, and I felt a tightness in my chest— almost as if I couldn't breathe.

"It's your fault!" he screamed. His face was red with anger, but fear showed in his eyes. "What are we going to do? It's getting dark. If no one finds us soon, who knows what will happen. There might be wolves or bears or even criminals hiding in these woods."

At the time, we had no idea that a suspicious person really was there in the woods.

Then Ronny started putting all the blame on me. "It's your fault," he accused again.

Quickly I remembered a wonderfully comforting thought. "Ronny," I said, "we'll be okay. God is watching over us. He knows where we are."

The suspicious onlooker had also been following us and was watching our every move. It wasn't until later that we found out about it. No telling what Ronny would have done, had he had a clue.

For the moment, I had to find another strategy. "Get out your compass. Remember? You said no one can get lost if he has a compass."

"Yeah, that's right," Ronny said excitedly, and he pulled out the precious compass. Just seeing it made him feel better.

"What does it say?" I asked. "Which way is back to the camp?"

He looked at the compass and panicked again. "A compass tells which direction you're facing, but I don't know if the camp is north or south or east or west. We're still lost." He jammed the compass back into his pocket and started accusing me again. "If you hadn't talked me into chasing that squirrel, we wouldn't be lost, . . . buddy." Then he burst into tears.

Lord, show me what to do, I prayed. *Think, Pudge! Think!*

Then I remembered what Grandfather Resource had taught me. "Stay in one place. If you start walking, you'll probably go in circles. If you stay in one place, someone will eventually find you."

"I'm sorry, Ronny. It is my fault we're lost," I said. "We never should have chased that squirrel, and I knew better than to get out of sight of Mr. Friendson. He's probably looking for us now."

The forest was darker than ever. "Listen," whispered Ronny nervously. "What's that noise?"

I listened. "You mean that buzzing noise?"

"Yes," he whispered again.

"I think it's cicadas. Just cicadas," I answered in a low voice while trying to sound calm.

"Will they eat us?"

At that, I felt some relief. "No, they're just insects. They won't hurt us."

Ronny let out a big sigh. He seemed to be calming down.

"Wait!" I said. "Do you hear that?"

"What?"

"Just listen." We stood quietly for a second, listening intently to the night sounds that were beginning to fill the woods. Then we both heard it as clear as anything. *Jing-a-ling-a-ling-a-ling.*

"The dinner bell!" we shouted together, and it didn't sound far away. Like a "shot out of a gun," as Pastor Gentle would have said, we ran toward the sound. Over a little rise, we tripped over our bags of pine cones. That sent us rolling on the ground. We were half laughing, half crying with relief and joy.

"You're a good buddy after all, Pudge. I'm sure glad you were with me."

"Not as good as the Lord, Ronny. God's Word says, 'I am with thee, and will keep thee in all places.' He was with me all the time, Ronny. Don't you see that you need Him too?"

"Yeah, I did think about it back there, Pudge, but I don't need Him now. Come on! Let's get to supper. We don't want to be late."

Had we been listening very closely at that moment, we might have heard a deep sigh back in the dark woods. It was a sigh that meant someone was glad we had found our way back. It was also a sigh of relief that, for now, no one seemed the wiser about his being there or about the strange things that had been happening around Camp Friendship.

CHAPTER 6

WHIPPED CREAM ON TOP

The dinner bell was still ringing as Ronny and I, dragging two big bags of pine cones, staggered up to the Dining Hall. Some wonderful smells greeted us, and Mr. Friendson met us at the bottom of the steps. "Mr. Thriftmore needed a little help, and I lost track of you two for a while. I was about to come after you."

"We had a little adventure, but the Lord helped us," I said.

"Well, you can tell me about it later. Right now, run up to the washroom and clean up a bit. I'll just carry these pine cones inside. That's where we need them anyway. We'll wait for you, but no more than five minutes."

That Mr. Friendson. He was letting a watch run his life—and ours; nevertheless, we straggled through the Dining Hall door four minutes and fifty-eight seconds later. Everyone was singing "Come and Dine," with Pastor Gentle leading.

"Better late than never," he said, glancing in our direction. We found our seats, and Pastor Gentle said the blessing. "Lord, thank You for this food and those who prepared it. Thank You for the privilege of being in these lovely surroundings at Camp Friendship. Thank You, also, for the opportunity to serve You by helping Aunt Ruth and Uncle Jake in this camp ministry. Amen."

When I opened my eyes and the aromas had fully teased my sense of smell, I began to think camp life at Camp Friendship was not so bad after all. If the lodges left something to be desired, the Dining Hall, quaint as it was, made a nice contrast.

At one end of the long room, the opposite end from the kitchen, was a huge fireplace that nearly filled the whole wall. It seemed this fireplace was what heated the room. It was built of stones, which were dark from the heat of many fires. Black iron tools hung to one side, and firewood was stacked in a rectangular opening on the other side. The mantel was high, and the fireplace opening seemed cavernous. I thought a boy my size could almost walk into it. A fire was crackling on the grates, and a big basket heaped with pine cones sat on the hearth. I found out later that they were used to help get the fire going. I wasn't cold now, but I would be very grateful for a fire the next morning.

Two rows of picnic tables covered with brightly patterned vinyl tablecloths had been placed side by

side down the room. Eight people could sit at each table; and, doing some quick math, I figured that sixty-four people could sit down at one time. From this, I assumed the camp had hosted quite a gang of campers over the years. Many young lives had obviously been touched. Mr. Friendson and Mr. Virtueson were just two that I knew personally. Our group sat at the two tables nearest the kitchen.

One quick glance around and I saw that the windows were sparkling, and the bare pine floor was freshly swept and oiled. We had done a good job. Soft polka-dotted curtains hung at the eight windows. The curtains looked so clean that I suspected the girls had gotten them from somewhere and had hung them during our chore time.

Having quickly surveyed the perimeter of the room, I could then concentrate on the center of the table. There were two big bowls of steaming stew, which was made of large chunks of meat, stubby carrot pieces, some celery slices, and pieces of potato and onion. The aroma was heavenly, and I could hardly wait until one bowl came my way. In the meantime, I helped myself to the freshly baked yeast rolls. There was spread, which turned out to be real butter, and several kinds of jams, which tasted to me like homemade. Grandmother Resource's jams couldn't have tasted any better to me at that moment. We each had a glass of what turned out to be raspberry tea, and we also had a bowl of garden salad with curly endive. The salad looked oily, so I assumed the dressing was already on it. Endive or not, I was hungry, and it tasted good. Finally, the stew came to me, and I loaded my plate and dug in.

We were all cramming our food down like we hadn't eaten for a month, and I noticed that Racer was using his Super Sport instead of regular silverware. *That's neat,* I thought.

Ronny nudged me in the ribs with his elbow and said in a low voice, "Look at him. He thinks he is so smart because he has that Super Sport. My compass is ten times better, don't you think?"

I didn't have a chance to answer him because Mr. Friendson asked, "Do all of you like the stew?"

"Yes!" we answered enthusiastically. Having worked so hard, I thought I could have eaten possum stew.

"I'm glad you like it," he said. "It's venison stew. There are a lot of deer around here."

"You mean we're eating a deer?" gasped Susie. "Those beautiful creatures."

"I don't care if it's moose or even bear," countered Mr. Thriftmore. "It is delicious."

Little more was said while we scraped our plates clean. It was wonderful to have a full stomach. If we had only known how hungry someone in the dark woods felt! Could he smell the savory stew and the yeasty hot rolls?

When nearly everyone was finished, Mr. Friendson stood up and blew that shocking whistle again. Not very loudly though. He knew Aunt Ruth and Uncle Jake were having their supper in the kitchen. I wondered if they had always been so lonely. Was that why they operated this camp? So they could have young people like us around?

"We're on a retreat, but we're going to follow camp rules just the same," announced Mr. Friendson. "Organization can help us all.

"Each person pass your plate to that end of the table." He was pointing to the kitchen end. "The last person on the far side gets to scrape everything onto one plate. Pass your silverware down to the person on the other side."

I felt so blessed. I wasn't sitting in either spot.

"For now, keep your forks. We do have dessert coming. You have all worked hard. You deserve this treat."

Dessert! Yes, I could certainly handle that. I wondered what it would be. *Will it be apple pie? Or chocolate ice cream?*

J. Michael shot up his hand. "What kind of dessert?"

Mr. Friendson smiled broadly. "Rhubarb pie! My camp favorite."

Wow! This is different, I thought. *Venison stew and rhubarb pie.*

"Those of you with the dirty dishes and silverware, carry them to the kitchen," continued Mr. Friendson, "and the cook will give you a stack of clean saucers and the cut pies. We may even get some whipped cream for the top. Yum!"

While Miriam and Sandy, Booker and Ace, and Mr. Thriftmore and Miss Content were getting the dessert, Mr. Friendson said, "I hope both lodges have lots of wood inside for the night. It may rain off and on, and wet wood does not burn. Tomorrow the sun should be out again, but tonight we'll probably have some rain."

I thought how nice it would be if we had our sleeping bags right here in the Dining Room and could stretch out in front of that big fireplace. The very thought was making me sleepy. How could I know that someone else longed for that fireplace too? His night would not be very comfortable, what with the weather predictions. But he was used to it, as I found out later.

My head was beginning to nod when the whistle blew again. "I'm going to let you 'hit the sack' early tonight," said Mr. Friendson. "You've had a big day, and we have a big day ahead tomorrow. But first we will finish supper."

Finish supper, I thought. *We just had dessert.*

"The dishes must be washed, the floor swept, and the tables wiped off."

I caught myself thinking some wrong thoughts. My attitude needed some cleaning up. I knew it, but I fought the uncomfortable feeling with a little selfish reasoning. *It has been a long day. We have worked so hard, and I'm tired.*

"We help keep expenses down when we do more of the work," explained Mr. Friendson. "Now, to be fair, those who scraped dishes and carried in the dessert get the easier jobs."

"That's not fair," complained Susie. "I would have gladly scraped dishes to keep from washing them."

"Excellent," declared Mr. Friendson. "Tomorrow, for breakfast, you can scrape and you won't have to wash dishes."

"I'm tired," grumbled Ronny, "and besides, I'm a guest. I should have special privileges."

"Not at Camp Friendship, Ronny. Everyone is treated the same, and everyone pulls his share of the load." Mr. Friendson gestured in Pastor Gentle's direction for support. "Right, Pastor?"

"That's right. 'If any would not work, neither should he eat,' and I didn't say that. The Scripture tells us. It's a Biblical principle."

Miss Content spoke up. "Come on, girls. We'll show them how it's done. To the kitchen. Forward! March!" Even Susie went along, but she was mumbling under her breath.

Actually, with all of us pitching in, we finished in a very short time. Oh, we were tired, but again, it was fun to work together.

CHAPTER 7

EARLY TO BED

When supper **was** finished and with drill sergeant Mr. Friendson leading the way with his flashlight, we all trudged out of the Dining Hall and headed toward our lodges. Warmth and security were left behind as the night surrounded us. The air was quite cool now, and the cicadas had stopped singing. A gentle mountain wind whispered in the tops of the pines, while leaves rustled on the ground below. A soft thump—now and then—indicated a pine cone or an acorn had just fallen.

From the far, far distant valley, we could faintly hear the lonesome wail of a train whistle. The sound only made my empty spot for home feel bigger.

Someone else at Camp Friendship also heard the whistle. Instead of bringing thoughts of home, though, it brought feelings of distress and regret. Hopping freight trains and riding the rails had seemed an exhilarating adventure for a while. But now, having to scavenge for food and always wondering what danger lurked in every dark place did not seem so attractive. No wonder such living was called a "hobo jungle."

As I told you, I didn't know anything about the interloper. All I knew was that Camp Friendship at night was nothing like Highland City. There were no street lights, and I kept myself from looking too far into the dark woods. I thought I might see eyes shining back at me. A pair of eyes was looking at us, and they were full of disappointment and sadness. Every person with a rebellious spirit eventually comes to feel that way.

Once we passed the stand of pines, I could see lights up ahead. One burned inside each washroom, and a floodlight served as a beacon for each lodge. The light was comforting, but the tar-paper blackness of the lodges was nearly lost in the surrounding darkness. The lodges definitely looked cold and deserted. Thoughts of that cold, musty-smelling room and a chilly sleeping bag were not very welcoming. *Why couldn't someone have gone ahead and built a fire in the potbellied stove?* I thought. There I was in a complaining mood again.

The only familiar thing was the night sky. Sometimes the trees opened up, and we could see a few stars dimly twinkling.

"Did you ever wonder what the night sky must look like to God when He looks down on it from Heaven?" Sandy asked of no one in particular.

"I think God sees right through it and sees us," answered Miss Content. "We are so insignificant and small in this universe, and yet God always sees us— each one of us. He cares about where we are and what we're doing, and He loves us."

"How great God is," Miriam said quietly.

"Maybe," mumbled Susie hard-heartedly.

No matter what Susie said, it certainly was something to think about, and we all walked along quietly, the pine needles soft under our feet.

When we came to the fork in the path, Mr. Friendson said, "Reginald, will you please come with me? Let's walk the ladies to their lodge."

"Yes, sir. It will be my pleasure to help you escort the girls to Queen Esther's Lodge," he replied with swelling chest. He even held out his elbow so Miss Content could take his arm.

Mr. Thriftmore had his flashlight, so he led the rest of us off toward David's Hideaway Lodge. We followed closely behind him in the inky darkness. The rest of us had left our flashlights in the lodge.

The moon was skipping in and out from behind a few wispy clouds. J. Michael said it was a waning moon. We took his word for that. All I noticed was that it had a hazy ring around it.

"What's wrong with it?" asked Ronny, gazing upward and almost tripping over a small tree branch the two of us had probably missed earlier. "It looks sick."

J. Michael shared more information. "The hazy ring can sometimes be a prediction of inclement weather," he noted with his usual intellectual authority. "As I must remind you, Mr. Friendson warned that we might have intermittent rain showers tonight."

"Oh, you and Reginald always have an answer," accused Ronny. "Why do you think you know it all? Maybe there is just fog on the moon tonight."

That was Ronny, my buddy for the weekend. *Why did he always have to be stirring up trouble, and why did he always have a bad attitude?* I thought. Then, my conscience gave me another jab. My attitude had not been the best either.

"But the moon has no atmosphere," protested J. Michael. "Therefore, it can't have fog."

Mr. Thriftmore knew it was time to intervene. "Boys, we'll have this discussion sometime later."

By now, Pastor Gentle was puffing his way up the sharp ridge to David's Hideaway. For a moment, I almost thought I could smell the faint scent of wood burning. That, too, brought thoughts of home. I remembered the same smell from my neighborhood. Not that sweet smell of someone's barbecue on a hot summer evening—more like what you smell on a cold, snowy night when the neighbors are burning logs in their fireplaces. Somewhere, someone had a toasty fire. I wished I were there.

The chill of the night air was getting to all of us, I suppose. "I think it is going to be cold tonight," said Racer. "Mom made me bring an extra blanket. I think I'm going to be glad I brought it."

"We have extra blankets for anyone who needs them," remarked Pastor Gentle between huffs and puffs. "'Always be prepared,' I say."

"Thank you for thinking ahead," said Ace. "I think we will all need extra blankets tonight."

Ronny piped up again. "Not me. I'm tough!"

In the shadows, our observer heard Ronny's remark and whispered under his breath, "How foolish, young man. I know, because I said the same thing myself fourteen years ago."

"Well, I for one do not like to be cold," said J. Michael. "By the way, is the washroom heated, Pastor? It's going to be cold taking showers tomorrow morning."

"The washroom is heated, and the lodge will be toasty warm tonight. I'll bank the fire and then get up before you boys in the morning. Don't worry. We'll be fine." His looking out for us really made me feel much more secure.

Having passed the washroom, we were soon at the lodge, and Mr. Thriftmore opened the door. Even before he could flip the light switch, we could see a red glow coming from the potbellied stove!

"Who built the fire?" asked Booker. We were all surprised.

"How pleasant," remarked Mr. Thriftmore. "Did you do this, Pastor Gentle?"

"Yes, I had to bring my sleeping bag and things, so Mr. Friendson and I came up here while everyone was finishing up at the Dining Hall. I guess no one missed us. Anyway, we started the fire then so the lodge could warm up."

I was liking him better all the time.

"Thank you, Pastor Gentle," said Ace. "We really appreciate it."

The room was comfortably warm. The fire in the potbellied stove had transformed a dark, cold, musty-smelling room into a cozy cabin . . . and I was very glad to see the bats were gone.

"Too bad the girls don't have a nice warm lodge," said Hapford. He was as kindhearted and caring as Pastor Gentle.

"Oh, they do. We started a fire for them also. I hope they'll be as pleased as you are."

"I'm sure they will," said Mr. Thriftmore. "Now, boys, get into your night clothes."

"Yes," added Pastor Gentle. "'Early to bed, early to rise,' I always say."

Mr. Thriftmore smiled. He knew Pastor Gentle was thinking what he was thinking—it wasn't going to be easy to get us settled down for the night. "Buddies can take turns going to the washroom before devotions," he said. Then, knowing our competitive natures, he had an idea to motivate us. "Okay, which buddies can set a record getting ready for bed?"

Ronny took the challenge eagerly. "Come on, Pudge. Let's beat them!"

I don't know how, but the two of us did manage to win. The fact that most of our clean clothes were dragged out onto the floor in the scramble didn't seem important.

"We're first!" yelled Ronny, bouncing on his bunk. That was important to him. For a second, I also thought it was pretty great to be first. Then I remembered what being first meant in this case. We would be the first to go out in the cold—and in the dark—to the washroom.

"Come on, Pudge, let's go," Ronny continued urging. "Reginald is letting us use his flashlight." He flipped on the strong beam and practically dragged me out the door.

Just by the way he held that flashlight, I knew he envied Reginald. As Pastor Gentle would have said, Ronny's compass "didn't hold a candle" to that flashlight, but I knew Ronny would never have admitted it. His compass was very special to him.

As we stepped outside in our bathrobes, I shivered, but it wasn't just from the chilly air. I didn't know why, but I had a feeling someone was watching us, and you know why now, don't you? Ronny and I hurried to the washroom, which, as Pastor Gentle had promised, was warm and well-lighted. We took our time inspecting the place and brushing our teeth. Finally we headed back. Actually the distance was only a few yards, but there were dark woods on both sides of the short, steep path. Was I ever glad we had Reginald's flashlight! It reminded me that Jesus is the Light of the world. I am so glad I have His light in my life.

We were almost to the lodge when, off to the left . . . SNAP! Ronny was leading and carrying the flashlight, of course. When he heard the snap, he automatically jerked the flashlight around toward it, shining the bright beam into the trees. A set of glowing eyes blazed back at us.

"A bear!" screamed Ronny. He tore off to the lodge, leaving me in the blackness. I yelled, and Mr. Thriftmore came running with his flashlight. We heard some crashing through the brush, and when he shined the light in that direction again, we caught a glimpse of the white, raised tail of a deer.

About that time Mr. Friendson came running up the path.

"What's the matter?" he asked breathlessly. "I heard screaming."

When Mr. Thriftmore explained, all Mr. Friendson said was, "Well, I'm not surprised. I said there were plenty of deer around here. The poor thing was probably just looking for a place to bed down for the night."

"Ronny said it was a bear," explained Booker. His eyes were big, and so were all the other boys' eyes.

Mr. Friendson continued to reassure us. "Like I said before, I really doubt there are any bears around here."

Well, I, for one, realized Mr. Friendson was not positive there were none. Maybe what we'd just met was not a bear, but that didn't mean there were no bears in these mountains. After all, something had broken into the kitchen and Camp Office. The way I reasoned, that would take something strong and clever—like a bear.

I really don't know if Pastor Gentle had it planned or whether he changed his topic because of the circumstances. But after everyone had finished his trip to the washroom and we were settled down, the devotion consisted of each of us reading a Scripture verse telling us either to "fear not" or to "be not afraid."

Reading these verses was good mental exercise after our encounter with "bears." It was the best bedtime medicine possible.

Finally we crawled into our sleeping bags, the fire was banked, and Mr. Friendson turned out the lights. A quiet hush came over the lodge. What a day! I tried to count how many times I had had to claim God's promises. As I thought about the curvy road, being lost in the woods, and bears, I went over in my mind the Scripture verses we had read in devotions. God saying "Fear not" really did make me feel calm and safe. Again I thought how wise Pastor Gentle was to give us those verses to sleep on.

I did wonder what Ronny was thinking. He had really been afraid several times, but he did not have the Lord in his heart to comfort him.

I was almost asleep when I heard sweet voices singing a chorus we had recently learned. "How can I fear? Jesus is near. He ever watches over me." It sounded like angels, but I never heard the rest of the song because I fell asleep before the song was finished. Evidently Miss Content had also found a way to reassure Sandy, Christi, Susie, and Miriam.

CHAPTER 8

THE HOOTING

I opened my eyes with a start. It was dark and the place was unfamiliar. I didn't know where I was, but someone was calling my name.

"Pudge, Pudge!" the voice called in a sharp whisper.

Then I remembered. This was Camp Friendship. I was sleeping with my friends in a lodge in the middle of the woods. Whose voice was that? Ace's? Booker's?

"Wa-a-ke up!" the voice called again with emphasis.

I still wasn't awake enough to answer. I had to get my senses about me first. Raising myself just a little on one elbow, I blinked and looked around. The old potbellied stove still glowed warmly, but that was the only light except for what came through the window. There, I could see the moon was still playing tag with the clouds, and it still had that hazy ring around it.

Ronny was whispering hoarsely. "Some buddy you are, Pudge."

I turned toward the voice. I couldn't see a face—it was too dark—but I whispered back. "What's the matter? You're going to wake up the others."

"I don't care," he said desperately but still whispering. "Listen! Do you hear that?"

Although I was still groggy, the way he said "Listen" made me take notice. What had Ronny heard? Why was he so frightened? Suddenly I was fully awake and listening.

I heard a soft scratching on the roof. I stiffened a little, then relaxed and lay back on the cot. The sound was familiar.

"It's just some tree branches scraping against the roof and side of the lodge," I explained. "That's all. Go to sleep."

"No, not that," he said emphatically.

Before he could say more, an eerie, goosebump-raising sound pierced the air. It was something between a howl and a hoot.

"Who-o, who-o-o."

A big chill went up my spine. I recognized that sound. I'd heard it once before when I was visiting Grandfather Resource on his houseboat. I didn't like it then, and I liked it even less now in the dark woods and lodge. Only one creature made that sound. It was a big-eyed, mysterious, old hoot owl, and it was nearby. I wriggled down deeper into my sleeping bag. Ronny was scared, and I didn't know

how much help I'd be. I pulled the edge of my sleeping bag tightly up to my chin.

"It's only an owl," I said, trying to sound as calm and brave as possible.

In the darkness I thought I heard a gulp. I couldn't see them, but I was sure Ronny's eyes were as big as tennis balls.

I swallowed hard and rambled on. "I saw a stuffed one in a museum once. They live in many forests, but they also live near the river where Grandfather ties up his houseboat. That was where I first heard one." I hoped that would be some comfort to him. Then, for some reason, I added, "They only come out at night. In the daytime they sleep."

"At night, huh. What do they eat?" asked Ronny.

Why did he have to ask that? "Mice and other rodents. That's what Grandfather said."

Where we were, inside the lodge, the only sound to be heard was soft snoring; but from outside we could still hear, every few moments, that clear, baleful "Who-o, who-o-o." It was unearthly, and I felt another chill.

I knew Ronny was frightened. I was his buddy, and I was supposed to help him.

"An owl won't hurt you," I said, as much to myself as to Ronny. "The sound is creepy," and it certainly was, "but he can't get inside. Now try to go to sleep. I'm right here and so are Mr. Friendson, Pastor Gentle, and Mr. Thriftmore."

"Who-o, who-o-o." There it was again, and it sounded even more creepy. The hair on the back of my neck stood straight up.

"That owl is scaring me, Lord," I softly prayed.

The Lord is wonderful. When we know Him, we can call on Him anytime. He is just waiting to help us—not always in the way we want Him to, but in the way that is best for us. At that moment, I wanted the owl to go away, but the Lord did something better for me.

Immediately I remembered the verses we had read in devotions just a few hours earlier. "Fear not; for I am with thee . . ." and "Fear not; I will help thee." I took a deep breath and felt better. God's promises were true, and no hoot owl could change that. Why should I be afraid? I wasn't alone. God was with me. He was watching over me. Yes, it was good to know the Lord.

Then a not-so-pleasant thought struck me. Ronny did not know the Lord. He could not claim the promises of God's Word as I could. That was the reason he was afraid, and I couldn't make his fear go away. I wanted to be a good buddy, but what could I do?

"Are you afraid too, Pudge?" Ronny's voice was weak and trembling. "What do **you** do when you're afraid?" he asked.

Then I knew what I could do to help him. It was important that I give the right answer, and again I asked the Lord to help me.

"I think about my favorite verses of Scripture, and I pray. Don't you want to know the Lord too, Ronny?" I asked quietly.

Ronny was still for a few moments. I waited for him to say something. He was obviously thinking very hard about this. He was struggling not only with his fear of the hoot owl, but also with the idea of giving his life to the Lord. Finally he said, "No, not now. I have to think some more about it. Maybe tomorrow I'll talk with Pastor Gentle. Thanks, Pudge. I'm glad you are here, and I'm glad I picked you for my buddy."

I was glad he'd picked me too. It had given me an opportunity to talk with him about the Lord, and I was thankful for the hoot owl. God has all kinds of ways of letting us know He loves us.

"Who-o, who-o-o." There was that haunting call again, but it wasn't scary for me anymore. God had used that old hoot owl to help me know the power of His Word, and to Ronny it was His voice saying, "Come unto Me."

I was almost asleep when I heard Ronny's soft, trembling whisper from the next cot. "God, I'm afraid. Help me go to sleep and not be afraid. Tomorrow I'll ask Pastor Gentle what I need to do so I can know You and not be afraid anymore."

Finally Ronny realizes he needs the Lord, I thought. *Hurray! Hurray!*

I prayed that he would remember and that he would talk with Pastor Gentle the next day. I peacefully dropped off to sleep. So did Ronny.

CHAPTER 9

AN UNINVITED VISITOR

In the cold, damp woods that surrounded David's Hideaway Lodge and Queen Esther's Lodge, the uninvited visitor, who had been watching all day, sat alone on an old tree stump. He was miserable in soul, and the cold and darkness didn't help. He was a man of about thirty-five, but he looked older. He had deep wrinkles in his forehead, and his shoulders slumped. His hair had grown long and gray. He had a shaggy beard and wore clothes that looked old and tattered. For sure, he was very lonely, dejected, and broken in spirit.

Camp Friendship was a place that was familiar to him, or had been. You might say he had grown up with it. Over the years it hadn't changed much. The old army barracks, covered in black tarpaper, looked as drab as ever. The dinner bell still rang to announce meals; the big fireplace still warmed the Dining Hall on cold, damp days. Uncle Jake still wore his camouflage cap, and Aunt Ruth wrapped herself in a shawl. The forked path still led to the lodges that nestled on top of the little ridge, and pine needles and pine cones cluttered the ground where the squirrels protested the invasion of noisy humans. The pines and other trees were taller now, but the woods were as thick and beautiful as ever.

The new washrooms were the only difference he could see. He remembered when the campers had carried water to the lodges and washed up in basins. If you wanted hot water, you had to heat it on the potbellied stove. Showers were an unknown luxury.

There had once been two additional lodges. Evidently they had crumbled from lack of repair and had been torn down. Actually, they were not needed because large groups of young people didn't come to Camp Friendship anymore. Churches that had once given their support had lost the vision for this mountain retreat. Now, they sent their boys and girls to camps where there were horseback riding, expansive athletic facilities, and fancier accommodations. There was nothing especially wrong with that, but nothing could replace the character-building experiences of Camp Friendship. But who was he to condemn anyone? Had he seen the score of opportunities at Camp Friendship when he was a young man? No.

Back then there had also been a log cabin hidden among the trees down a path from the Camp Office.

Aunt Ruth and Uncle Jake had built the cabin as their rustic home—right there on the land they had purchased for a youth camp ministry. It had been a pleasant, comfortable, airy home full of laughter and love. Now, because of their advancing years, Aunt Ruth and Uncle Jake lived in a little room at the back of the Camp Office. Most of the time they sat on the porch rocking and observing others around the camp. He wondered if they remembered or ever thought of him. The highlights of their lives now seemed to be only the buses—like the one from Highland Church—that rolled up occasionally with a group of boisterous, enthusiastic young people.

That night, as he shivered beside his small campfire, under a discarded scrap of tarpaulin that he had found near David's Hideaway, he thought about the old cabin that surely must still be standing. It was probably in sad shape. He could no doubt find shelter there from the cold and rain that was likely to come that night. It was only a thought, a consideration. He would not feel comfortable there. He would rather put himself at the mercy of the elements. That was certainly nothing new for him.

The last two nights he had slept in David's Hideaway. He had found an unlocked window and had crawled in. It was musty and dusty, but better than sleeping outdoors. As he shivered again, he felt the loneliness that often came over him; and now, sleeping outside, he related to the dejected Bible hero for whom the lodge was named. King David had been on the run and so was he. The only difference was that David in the Bible had been running from his enemies, while he was running from God and from himself.

Sometime after the lights had gone out in the lodges, he had crept closer and peered through the newly cleaned windows. In the darkness, he could barely see the faces of the exhausted young boys scrunched down in their sleeping bags. In his mind he was testing them. Would they pass the test, or would they fail, just as he had? It was a glum thought, which broke off as he heard the heavy snoring of Pastor Gentle. What a man! He had not changed a bit over the years.

The soft glow of the potbellied stove warmed the visitor's soul, if not his body, and more pleasant thoughts crept in. He couldn't help but chuckle when he reviewed what he had observed that day—the bat incident, the lizards, the adventure in the woods, and, of course, the scramble just a little earlier outside the boys' washroom. Little did the boys know that they had startled not only a deer but him as well. He had almost been caught in the beam of that super flashlight.

The man's stomach growled, reminding him of how hungry he was. He would break into the kitchen again and eat some leftovers before he crawled into his makeshift bed and tried to get some sleep. One of the repairs that day had been to fix the lock on the kitchen door. He would have to try a window or figure out another way to get in.

CHAPTER 10

BRIGHT THINGS AHEAD

"Twe-e-e-et!!!"

Before any of us could believe it, the shrillness of Mr. Friendson's whistle shocked us wide awake.

"Time to get up, boys," he announced too enthusiastically.

"Twe-e-e-et!!!" Our sleepy brains rattled again.

"Come on. Roll out," he ordered. He was being our drill sergeant again.

Still huddled in my warm sleeping bag, I looked out the window again. The moon was gone and it was light now, but the sun wasn't up. There was water dripping from the eaves, and the sky looked misty. Just as Mr. Friendson had predicted, we had obviously had a light rain in the early morning hours after Ronny and I had had our conversation. Now that whole episode seemed almost like a dream. Had Ronny really prayed and promised to talk with Pastor Gentle about receiving Christ?

"Twe-e-e-et!!! First buddies up get the showers first."

Pastor Gentle could not pass up the occasion to offer another word to the wise. "Remember, 'The early bird catches the worm.'" He stoked the fire and threw in more wood. The room still had a definite chill, though.

"Is there ever an occasion for which your pastor does not have a saying to fit?" Racer quietly asked Booker.

"I doubt it. That's what I like best about him. I'm going to try to remember his sayings as I grow up."

None of us were in any big hurry to crawl out and put our feet on the cold floor. I noticed Mr. Thriftmore was just coming back from the washroom. Seeing him, the thought of going out into the raw, damp air to take a shower was even less appealing.

None of the "roughing it" seemed to bother Mr. Friendson. He marched right over to Queen Esther's Lodge to blow his whistle and make sure the girls were up. The "Twe-e-e-et!!!" was as annoying as a foghorn on this misty, dreary morning, and it didn't promise to be a great day. The one bright spot was that Ronny was going to talk to Pastor Gentle. I wondered when he would do it.

As I said, none of us were in a big hurry to get up, but Ace and J. Michael were first, then Hapford and Reginald. As Ace and J. Michael came shivering back from the washrooms, Booker and Racer stepped out onto the cold floor and went to the potbellied stove to put on their robes and slippers. Eventually, Ronny and I got up and found a place by the stove also, while we waited our turn for the washroom. By the time we headed there, the lodge was snugly warm, and Ace and J. Michael were dressed and rolling up their sleeping bags. The others were in various stages of getting ready for breakfast.

Naturally, since Ronny and I were the last to the showers, we did not get **hot** showers. The water started out slightly warm and quickly went to br-r-r cold. I think I set a record for taking the fastest shower. I grabbed my robe and slippers and quickly headed back to the lodge. Ronny was right behind me.

"I wonder who got the cold showers at Queen Esther's Lodge?" I said to Ronny as we hurried up the steep path. We never heard, but at breakfast we found out what did happen. It was even more exciting and unexpected.

Susie got the first shower, and she took her "pets" with her . . . except she lost one in the shower. She didn't warn anyone either. Maybe she didn't even realize she had lost one. At any rate, Christi found it later when she took her shower.

Christi's blood-curdling scream must have scared it, because it skittered away before Susie could catch it. Later, Sandy found Susie's "pet," or one of its friends, in the sink when she was brushing her teeth. Then Miriam found one in her slipper when she put her foot in it. That lizard really got around, or it had a lot of curious friends. The way they changed color didn't help any. You could almost put your hand on one without even knowing it. When one escaped out the door, Susie wailed, "You killed my 'pet!' It will freeze to death out there—or starve!"

Miss Content was finally able to convince her that the lizard had gotten along just fine before Susie had rescued it. When the breakfast bell rang, she forgot all about the one lost "pet" and scooped up the others and put them in her jacket pocket.

During all that excitement at Queen Esther's Lodge, we boys were busy at David's Hideaway Lodge. We rolled up our sleeping bags and straightened up the lodge. Mr. Thriftmore made sure we did everything proper, and that we didn't forget anything we had shoved under our cots.

We heard the breakfast bell too, and when we opened the door, the sky had cleared and the sun was coming up. The air was still quite cold and very damp. We slipped and slid down the path on wet leaves and pine needles. Miss Content and the girls were laughing and chattering as they came from their lodge and met us at the fork. There was no time to talk about the events of the night before, the showers, or other adventures if we were to be on time for breakfast; and none of us wanted to be late for breakfast!

Once down the hill and into the clearing at the Dining Hall and Camp Office, we could see the sun just above the horizon.

Ronny found another occasion to use his compass.

"The sun is coming up in the east," he announced, as if that were some great revelation.

"Of course it's coming up in the east," declared Susie. "Everyone knows it always comes up in the east and sets in the west."

"Susie, you are so right," said Pastor Gentle.

She beamed proudly and glared at Ronny.

"Do you know why it always comes up in the east and sets in the west?" Pastor Gentle continued.

She wrinkled her nose as if to say, "Why did you have to spoil my moment of attention with some silly question?" Her look was disrespectful.

"Sunrise and sunset were planned by God," Pastor Gentle said, smiling. "They will never change, and it reminds us that none of God's laws ever change."

As the sun crept higher, the sky was a gorgeous red with streaks of glowing gold.

"Isn't it beautiful!" said Christi in awe.

Reginald raised his brows authoritatively. "Red sky in morning, sailors take warning," he noted.

"Oh, that's just a saying. It doesn't mean anything, Reginald," Sandy countered. "Besides, we're not at sea. We're on top of a mountain."

"I take exception to that," stated Reginald. He was not backing down. "I'm correct, am I not, Pastor Gentle?"

The kindly pastor put his hand on Reginald's shoulder and again smiled; then he answered thoughtfully. He was not about to be caught in the middle of such a serious discussion.

"Actually, there is truth in what both of you say. We are not at sea, and we certainly are on top of a mountain." He nodded to Sandy, and she smiled with just a hint of pleasure over being right. When the pastor turned to address Reginald, the corners of her mouth dropped a little.

He patted Reginald's shoulder again. "What you said, Reginald, is really a paraphrase of what Jesus once said to His disciples to teach them a lesson. There is also a scientific reason why a red sky in the morning may mean bad weather is ahead. I'd suggest that you do some further research on that subject when you get home."

"I'll do that, sir, and thank you for your kind remarks."

The discussion was over, and it was a good thing, because Mr. Friendson started blowing his whistle. We all trooped into the dining room.

As far as we could see, nothing had changed from the night before, but then, we hadn't been in the kitchen earlier when the cook spoke to Mr. Friendson. Another piece of the "missing food mystery" had presented itself. The cook was bumfuzzled (that means "confused"). There was definitely some food missing, but how did something or someone steal it?

"They must have pried open a window or picked the lock," the cook insisted to Mr. Friendson. "For sure, it was no raccoon or bear! I'll have to let the rangers and local police know about this."

At the time, no one had mentioned the missing food to Uncle Jake and Aunt Ruth, but Mr. Friendson quietly shared the news with Miss Content, Pastor Gentle, and Mr. Thriftmore. They didn't let on, and none of us found out about it until much later. We were too hungry to notice the concern on Mr. Friendson's face. Without a hint about the incident, he directed us to tables near the fireplace. Two tables were set again, and a stack of bowls stood proudly at the ends.

"The food will be out soon," he announced routinely

In the fireplace, logs were heaped high and were snapping and crackling their welcome. Bright coals glowed under the grate, and the toasty warmth quickly dried out the dampness we felt from our trek down from the lodges. It was really cozy, and I was so hungry I could have eaten . . .

Well . . . let me tell you about that. Do you remember earlier when I mentioned my vision of country ham and eggs, biscuits and gravy, and other country treats? Forget it. The main items for breakfast at Camp Friendship were either cornmeal mush with milk or oatmeal with milk. We didn't get a choice—Saturday morning it was oatmeal. My mom is the only one I know who can make good oatmeal, and the camp cook did not have my mom's recipe.

The biscuits rated high on my brag list. Hot from the oven, they were fluffy, high, and golden brown. Butter just melted on them, and there was plenty of homemade jam. Mr. Friendson said it was huckleberry jam made from huckleberries that grew in the valley in summer. I didn't care what kind of berries were in the jam; it was good. I decided to fill up on biscuits, and so did Booker and Racer.

Mr. Thriftmore didn't think filling up on biscuits was a very good idea though. "If you eat biscuits, you eat oatmeal too," he said. We did, and our stomachs were soon full.

The spy in the woods missed all this, although he probably suspected what was on the menu. Very little had changed over the years, including the breakfast menu. Since oatmeal, biscuits, and jam were out of the question—unless he slipped into the kitchen later—he would have to find his breakfast somewhere else. He knew just where, and thanks to Pastor Gentle, it wouldn't be too hard. He'd have to hurry, though, before Pastor Gentle came back to the lodge.

With breakfast over, it was clean-up time again. As promised, Susie got to scrape dishes and collect silverware. Oatmeal stuck to each spoon like peanut butter sticks to the roof of your mouth. She turned up her nose but never complained. She had learned the night before that complaining did not get her out of work. Besides, she had her buddy Miriam to help her.

I expected that Ronny might decide to talk with Pastor Gentle while we did our jobs. I would even have suggested it, but he didn't know I had heard his prayer. Before I could say anything, Ronny made a beeline to the kitchen, seemingly eager to "shoulder his share of the load," as Pastor Gentle would have said.

Now, oatmeal is hard enough to scrape, but try scrubbing it out of a pot or a pan! It sticks like glue and makes the dishrag and water feel slimy. Two of us got the job of scrubbing pots and pans. No, not Ronny and I. It was J. Michael and Ace. They never complained though. They started singing happy songs, and before long the job was done.

Again, teamwork got the clean-up job done quickly. While we were finishing, Mr. Friendson tooted his whistle again—not very loudly so as not to startle Aunt Ruth and Uncle Jake. Then he announced, "We'll be having a short Bible study with Pastor Gentle in exactly five minutes."

Will we ever be able to get away from time limits and that whistle? I wondered.

"We'll be going on a hike this morning, and, weather permitting," he continued, "we'll have a cookout for lunch."

"Can we make hobo stew?" asked Ace, drying his dishpan hands.

Mr. Friendson smiled. Remember, Ace had been to Camp Friendship before. *Hobo stew must be some special treat,* I thought, but the rest of us didn't have a clue. I, for one, did not want to ask.

"What's hobo stew?" Susie finally asked.

Ronny jumped on this opportunity to show his true character again. "It's stew made out of lizards," he snickered and nearly doubled over with laughter.

Susie glared at him and put her hands over the pocket where her "pets" were.

"That wasn't funny, Ronny," reprimanded Miriam. Her sweet, caring spirit made tears of sympathy begin to pool in her eyes. "It was mean."

"That's right," said Susie defensively. "Miriam is my buddy, and she will stick up for me. You're just sorry you don't have a pet."

"Children, children, please," interrupted Pastor Gentle. "This is Camp Friendship. Friends do not talk with malice, and they do not treat each other in this way."

I believe he was genuinely shocked at such behavior. He put one hand on Susie's head and one on Miriam's head and guided them back to the tables by the fireplace. He gave Ronny a disappointed look, and Ronny hung his head.

Maybe now he will realize how badly he needs to settle things with the Lord, I thought piously. Then I immediately felt guilty for thinking I was so much better than he was.

Ronny quickly shrugged off this incident as if nothing had happened. As far as I could see, he had no guilt about what he'd done and had passed off his prayer of the night before just as easily. I suppose that is how it is when someone says "No" to God again and again.

The amazing thing is that God is very patient and never stops loving us. It is continually His desire that we will trust Him and live for Him. Over and over, He makes a way for those who do not know Him to come to Him, and His arms are always open to meet the needs of His children. God is Love.

As we relaxed and got comfortable around the crackling fire, God was holding out His open, loving arms to a cold, hungry prodigal around a little campfire some distance away. That man had quite a battle going on inside. His heart said, "I'm tired of running; I want to go home." But reason said, "You have sinned too much; you have hurt too many people; you have said 'No' to God too many times. No one cares about you. You are not welcome at Camp Friendship anymore."

I didn't know what God was doing by the little campfire in the woods, and neither did any of the others. We just sat there, soaking up the warmth of the fire, waiting for Pastor Gentle to begin his devotion.

CHAPTER 11

THE PRESENT OF FRIENDSHIP

As we sat cross-legged on the floor and on benches around the fireplace, I noticed that buddies were sitting together. Something special was happening. We were all friends, but only a few of us had been close friends. The buddy system was helping us get to know one another better than before. It was helping us share feelings, plans, and special times. Maybe that was part of the reason for this retreat at Camp Friendship.

As Mr. Friendson, Mr. Thriftmore, and Miss Content also found places near the fire, Pastor Gentle cleared his throat and began. "I will read a Scripture verse from Proverbs, and then I want to tell you a special story.

"The verse says, 'Thine own friend, and thy father's friend, forsake not; neither go into thy brother's house in the day of thy calamity: for better is a neighbour that is near than a brother far off.'

"Now here's the story: Once there was a little boy about your age. We'll call him Joe. He had three sisters and one brother and a new baby brother or sister on the way. Joe was the oldest.

"His parents were God-fearing folks who were well-respected in the community. Nevertheless, the family was rather poor. They weren't poor because Joe's father didn't work hard. He did. Along with his trade he often did odd jobs around the community and in the nearby town. But with seven mouths to feed, things were always 'nip and tuck,' as you might say.

"They made do though, and they didn't think of themselves as poor. They always had a garden in the summer, Joe's mother sewed most of their clothes, and they got along with the necessities and an occasional luxury. They were Believers, and they were happy, loving, and satisfied with what God had given them.

"As I said before, Joe was the oldest. He was ten, nearly eleven, that year. It was close to Thanksgiving, and it was also close to the time for the new baby to be born. Of course, he hoped it would be a boy."

"Yeah, a boy is better," interrupted Ronny. He was really getting interested in the story.

Pastor Gentle didn't seem to mind the interruption. He just smiled at Ronny and winked at the girls. Then he continued. "Well, as I said, it was almost Thanksgiving. The new baby coming meant one more mouth to feed, and, of course, there would also be a hospital bill after the baby was born.

"Then, just a week before Thanksgiving, the family's old car broke down. It was a serious breakdown too, and not one that Joe's father could fix. They couldn't afford a new car, so Joe's dad agreed to do odd jobs at the repair shop to pay for what needed to be done to get the car back on the road. That was fine, except that it meant no extra income from other odd jobs for a while. The family really depended on those extra odd jobs, especially at that time of year and with the baby coming. The whole situation was something for which the family was not prepared.

"On Thanksgiving Day, although she was not feeling well, Joe's mother fixed Thanksgiving dinner. Since things were so 'nip and tuck' with the car repairs and the upcoming hospital bill, the family couldn't afford a turkey. Instead, Joe's mother stuffed a tough, old but fat, hen. It may not have been as much of a treat as turkey, but they were thankful for the stuffed chicken, and they were blessed with other Thanksgiving treats.

"When the family sat down to eat, Joe noticed that his mother did not look well. Before the meal was over, she asked Joe's father to take her to the hospital. It was time for the baby to be born. The children were dropped off at a neighbor's home on the way.

"The baby was born that night, and it was a little girl."

"Yes!" cheered the girls.

"Why couldn't it have been a boy, Pastor Gentle?" asked Ronny. "Are you playing favorites with the girls?"

Pastor Gentle laughed heartily. His chest shook up and down again. "No, Ronny. I'm not playing favorites. I said the baby was a girl because this is a true story."

"Hm-m-m," Racer whispered to Booker, "I didn't know he really knew these people. I thought he was making it up."

"May I continue now?" asked the pastor.

We all nodded or said "Yes, go on."

"The whole family was happy that the baby had arrived safely. However, a problem showed up the next day. The baby could not keep food down because a muscle in her stomach wasn't working properly. The doctor told Joe's parents that their baby would have to stay in the hospital until they could find the cause and come up with a treatment for the problem.

"Joe's mother and father prayed and gave the baby into the Lord's care. Still, it meant added medical expenses—expenses for which the family budget did not allow. Two days later Joe's mother came home, but the baby had to stay in the hospital.

"One week went by, then two. The doctors kept trying to get the baby to keep food down. Every day in the hospital meant the bill was adding up.

"Then, just two weeks before Christmas, Joe and his brother came down with chicken pox. They were miserable with the itching."

"O-o-oh, chicken pox!" exclaimed Christi. "That is possibly the worst thing that ever happened to me."

Those of us who had had it agreed, and we got Pastor Gentle off track with his story again while we swapped horror stories of our experiences.

"Children, let's allow Pastor Gentle to continue," suggested Miss Content. "I believe there must be a happy ending to this story and a lesson in it for all of us."

"Yes, Pastor, go on," said J. Michael. "We should not have interrupted."

The pastor continued, "At last Christmas Eve arrived. Just as Joe had expected, there were no presents to unwrap and enjoy. Although he knew there was no money for presents and he really didn't expect any, he was still quite sad. He hurt even more for his brother and sisters. They were younger and really did not understand. There had been hard Christmases before, but never one like this; and, as badly as Joe would have liked to buy presents for his brother and sisters, he didn't have any money.

"The family did have one tradition that neither lack of money nor chicken pox could affect. After the evening meal on Christmas Eve, Joe's father always read the Christmas story and the family sang Christmas carols.

"They were doing that and trying to forget that there was no money for the hospital bill or for any presents when someone knocked on their door.

"It was the same kind neighbor and his wife who had kept the children when their mother had gone to the hospital. They had their four-year-old son with them, and their faces were rosy with the crisp Christmas Eve cold. They were also loaded down with many brightly wrapped packages.

"Coming through the door into the warm living room, the man said, 'We know your family is going through some hard times just now. You have not complained or come begging. In fact, you have been

a wonderful Christian example to us. It's Christmas, and we want to share God's blessings with you. These are presents for the children and some money we've set aside. We want you to use it for the hospital bill.'

"Joe's father protested at first, but the neighbors insisted. Finally, Joe's father accepted that this was God's way of providing for his family. The children were excitedly talking about the beautifully wrapped presents when the phone rang. It was the doctor. Joe's little sister was well enough to go home, and they could pick her up in the morning. Part of the hospital bill did have to be paid though, and the Lord had just provided the money for it."

Pastor Gentle paused to catch his breath. "So, as Miss Content suggested, this story had a happy ending. On Christmas Day, Joe's new baby sister was finally home, and the family was all together. Because of the friendship and kindness of neighbors, Joe's father had the money to pay what the hospital required, and Joe and his brother and sisters all had gifts to unwrap and enjoy. It was truly the best Christmas Joe ever had.

"Remember the Scripture verse? 'Thine own friend, and thy father's friend, forsake not; neither go into thy brother's house in the day of thy calamity: for better is a **neighbour** that is near than a brother far off.'"

We all sat quietly for a few seconds, thinking about the story and how it illustrated the verse Pastor Gentle had read.

Ace spoke up first. "So, did you know Joe, Pastor Gentle?"

"I certainly did—and do," he answered. "You do too. In fact, you are so close to him you could touch him."

We all looked around and at each other. Mr. Thriftmore and Miss Content were looking at each other with as much puzzlement as the rest of us. Only Mr. Friendson and Pastor Gentle were smiling.

Suddenly Sandy stood up. "It's you, isn't it, Pastor Gentle? You were, or are, Joe?"

Again the lovable gentleman chuckled, and his chest shook up and down. "You are right, Sandy. I'm Joe."

"Then who are the kind neighbors?" asked Racer. "Do we know them?"

"I think you could say that," answered the pastor slyly. "Mr. Friendson, you tell them."

All heads turned to our retreat's drill sergeant. He had a knowing grin on his face, and he was gesturing toward the kitchen. "The kind neighbors were Aunt Ruth and Uncle Jake."

"Wow!"

"Really?"

Now we knew why Pastor Gentle had such admiration and respect for the older couple who found so much joy in sitting on the porch of the Camp Office and watching young people come and go around Camp Friendship. Their demonstration of true friendship had changed one little boy's life many years before, and their camp was changing our lives too.

"What happened to their little boy?" asked Booker with curious interest. "Why doesn't he help them run Camp Friendship?"

"That's another story," answered Mr. Friendson, "a very sad story. You see, their son David was my buddy every summer that I came to Camp Friendship. We were very close friends. I always thought we would be buddies in everything, but when I surrendered my life to the Lord for His service, things changed. David became rebellious because he was not willing to follow the Lord. He admitted to me that he thought God wanted him to work in the ministry here at Camp Friendship, but he didn't want to do that. He wanted to be happy and successful, and he was certain happiness and success could not be found in this ministry.

"Aunt Ruth and Uncle Jake have not heard from him in years. They have tried to find him and hoped he would contact them, but they have never been able to find him. They don't even know if he is alive or dead."

"How sad," commented Miss Content.

"It is very sad," agreed Mr. Friendson. "They have never given up hope, but only God knows what became of their boy. I still pray for him because he was my buddy."

CHAPTER 12

OFF WE GO

It seemed every hour at Camp Friendship revealed either something unexpected or a new adventure. Even the weather was surprising. One minute it was cloudy and misty, and the next the sun was shining and encouraging us to follow Mr. Friendson on some new escapade.

By the time Pastor Gentle had finished his story, the sun was sparkling through the Dining Hall windows. I guess we needed that after hearing about Aunt Ruth and Uncle Jake's son.

Mr. Friendson wasn't about to let us mope around. "Is everyone ready to go on our hike?" he asked. "Look how the weather has cleared. Let's thank the Lord for His goodness!" He looked toward Heaven, smiled, and grabbed his jacket. We had already had more than enough new experiences and adventures for one retreat. *How could anything more exciting happen on a hike?*

I had little time to think more about it because Mr. Friendson was already pumping our enthusiasm. "It's time we were getting started. We are going to follow a hiking trail laid out for campers; and, as I said at breakfast, we will have a cookout for lunch, weather permitting. I hope you all like hobo stew. That's what is on the menu."

I was hoping hobo stew would be more tasty than oatmeal, and I wondered what we'd use for dishes.

"Each of you should have a canteen," continued Mr. Friendson.

Ronny immediately threw up his hand and yelled, "I don't have one! Hapford didn't tell me to bring one." That was Ronny, all right. Always blaming someone else for his problems.

"No problem," said Mr. Friendson without a second thought. "I found two when we were cleaning the Camp Office yesterday. Each of you make sure yours is filled with clean water."

We all nodded, and Ronny seemed happy. He patted his pocket where he had his compass to make sure it was still there. He was set.

Mr. Friendson continued as he glanced around at our feet, "Do all of you have suitable shoes for hiking?"

I had noticed earlier that he had on heavy leather boots with thick soles. He had the cuffs of his pants neatly tucked down inside the high tops. They looked like just the thing for climbing over rocks, tree stumps, and logs. With his red plaid flannel shirt, Mr. Friendson looked more like a lumberjack than my Learning Center supervisor. I chuckled. Camp Friendship was changing all of us.

"Reginald, you look all set," he said as he continued glancing around the room. Reginald had similar boots, but he didn't have the cuffs of his pants tucked in.

"Thank you, sir. I believe suitable footwear is always a necessity." He bent over to tuck in his cuffs also. I suppose he was trying to model Mr. Friendson. I did admire the warm-looking sheepskin vest he had gotten especially for the trip.

Susie was not to be overlooked. "I got new tennis shoes just for this retreat," she boasted and lifted one foot to show off the fancy, expensive shoes. They had thick, wide soles and a strip of reflector tape on each heel. All the rest of us had on tennis shoes too.

"Those are very nice, Susie," said Mr. Friendson.

With a hug, Miriam added, "I am so glad you could get new shoes, Susie. I'm also glad we both came on this retreat." Sweet Miriam never seemed to hold a grudge, not even over finding lizards in her slippers.

Susie beamed. Things seemed to be going just as she wanted. She had gotten attention, and she had a buddy who truly treated her as a friend.

"You may want to put on an extra pair of socks to keep from getting blisters," suggested Mr. Friendson, glancing at our feet once again, "and make sure you have your jackets. It will be chilly when we are out of the sun and deep in the forest. If you brought a backpack, strap it on and bring along any of those small camping items we talked about on the bus. Don't forget that Super Sport, Racer. It will come in very handy. And keep your compass handy, Ronny. We certainly don't want to get lost."

I didn't think we'd get lost; but, at Mr. Friendson's comment, Ronny swelled with pride. The Super Sport had been getting enough attention. He just knew his compass was better camping gear.

"How far are we going to hike?" asked Christi.

"Far enough to work up a good appetite," said Mr. Friendson. "I have a special place in mind. It will be perfect for our cookout."

We were satisfied. That was all the information we needed.

"Now, to make our trip a little more interesting," he continued, "we're going to have a nature scavenger hunt along the way. I'm going to give each pair of buddies a list of things to collect." He held up a sheaf of papers. "Some will be easy to find, and others a little more difficult. Finding them all will take sharp eyes and even a little creativity, but they can be found. Just work together, and look beyond the obvious.

"These are some of the things you will be looking for," he added, pausing to read from one list, "a pine cone, an acorn, a red leaf, a yellow leaf, some moss, a wildflower, a fern, a feather, an empty bird's nest, an empty eggshell, . . ."

"A bird's nest is just what we need for making hobo stew," snickered Ronny. He looked to see if the girls had heard him. Sandy had, and the look on her face said she didn't think eating a bird's nest was a very good idea.

". . . a white stone, birch bark from a fallen branch, a needle, a caterpillar, . . ."

"O-o-o," choked Sandy. She pulled her mouth down at the corners, grabbed her throat, and puckered her brows in a deep furrow. "That's one Christi and I won't even look for."

"Do lizards count?" asked Susie happily. If so, she and Miriam already had a hcad start.

"Here are the lists. Check for yourselves." Moving from buddy to buddy, he started passing them out. "You may go back to the lodges and get anything you need for the hike. Meet me in front of the Camp Office in ten minutes." He grasped the whistle and puffed his cheeks as if he were going to blow it, but then he had second thoughts.

"Yes, sir," we all chimed, clicking our heels together and saluting. If he were going to be a drill sergeant, we were going to be good soldiers.

Ronny and I were the last ones to come running back when Mr. Friendson blew his whistle ten minutes later. Ronny had on his backpack, and, of course, he had his compass. I had to admit that it was an important piece of equipment for a hiker, and I was very pleased to be his buddy.

As we joined the others, I noticed that Aunt Ruth and Uncle Jake had already stationed themselves on the porch. Now and then they looked up and squinted approvingly over the tops of their glasses.

Before we were ready to leave, Mr. Friendson helped Mr. Thriftmore wrestle a large, insulated backpack up onto his shoulders. Mr. Friendson already had one strapped to his back. Pastor Gentle had the large pockets of his insulated jacket crammed full, which made him look uncomfortably stuffed. The thick, woolly hat that covered his balding head completed his outdoorsman look. He also had a long pole he was probably going to use as a walking stick and maybe a fishing pole.

Before we started off, Mr. Friendson and Mr. Thriftmore checked everyone's backpack to make sure we had proper jackets and full canteens.

As they were doing that, Pastor Gentle said to Ronny and me, "Did either of you see or happen to pick up my fishing line and hooks? I hung them on a nail outside the door of the lodge last night. I didn't want anyone lying or stepping on them. I forgot to see if they were there when we went to breakfast, but when we went back just now, the line and hooks weren't there."

"I didn't take them," popped back Ronny immediately. He was always ready to defend himself. "Why do you think I stole them?"

"I don't think you stole them," answered Pastor Gentle kindly. "I just thought you might have picked them up for me. We may find a stream today, and I thought I might see if I could catch a fish. Maybe I'm just starting to forget where I put things."

I really didn't think Ronny had taken the fishing line or the hooks, and, as it turned out, I was right. You know now who had, though—the interloper in the woods. He had used them to get his breakfast.

"Line up. Buddies together," ordered Drill Sergeant Mr. Friendson. "We're ready to march out."

There was no more time to fuss over the missing fishing line and hooks.

As we headed out, I whispered to Ronny, "Which way are we headed?"

He pulled out his compass and looked. "North," he answered. "That means we want to go south to come back." Having that compass really made him feel important.

Mr. Friendson, of course, was in the lead with Miss Content and the girls behind. Pastor Gentle followed them, and Mr. Thriftmore brought up the rear, with Ace and J. Michael, Booker and Racer, Hapford and Reginald, and Ronny and me in between.

"Twe-e-e-et!!!"

As we marched off, Aunt Ruth and Uncle Jake raised their hands and slowly waved us on. I wondered how many hundreds of groups of young people like us they had seen start out on hikes.

Meanwhile, our spy was just returning from catching his breakfast. He hung the line and hooks back on the nail outside the door of David's Hideaway Lodge. He could hear Mr. Friendson barking directions to us. Pastor Gentle started a chorus. "I have decided to follow Jesus. I have decided to follow Jesus . . . ." As our voices trailed off, the words brought tears to the man's eyes. How many times as a young man, just like Ronny, Ace, J. Michael, Booker, Racer, Hapford, Reginald, and me, had he sung those words? Many good, as well as painful, memories kept returning.

CHAPTER 13

BACK TO NATURE

As we headed out on the hiking trail, we were almost immediately in thick woods. It was like being in a different world. We were surrounded by tree trunks—all sizes and kinds. Most of the trees were bare or losing their leaves, but here and there was a stand of evergreens. Some were tall, magnificent pines with swishy long needles. Others were more like bushes with delicate, almost lacy branches. Pastor Gentle called them hemlocks.

Under the canopy of the large spreading branches were smaller trees struggling to reach the sun, as well as patches of brambles with their thorns bare now that fall had taken most of their leaves. Underfoot spread a gorgeous carpet of leaves in all the fall colors. The early morning showers had left them wet and slippery.

We happily tramped along, the wet leaves sticking to our shoes, twigs snapping and popping as we tromped on them. We often had to step over rotting tree trunks and trailing vines. All the summer wildflowers had disappeared, but now and then we did see a holly bush with its bright red berries.

Even our noses realized something was different. The sweet, smoky smell of logs burning in the fireplace was replaced with the damp, musty smell of dead leaves.

Sandy sneezed a few times. "I think I'm allergic to mold," she said. "There must be a lot of it in these woods."

"More than likely," said Pastor Gentle. "In summer you would smell honeysuckle, wild roses, and other wildflowers; but now it's dead leaves, wet wood, and moss. Once the sun has had an opportunity to dry things out, you won't notice it so much."

The forest was full of activity. Overhead, birds, chirping excitedly, flitted from branch to branch. I supposed they were warning their friends that we were coming. There was activity closer to the ground also—mostly squirrels. They were digging in the leaves and racing up tree trunks. Pastor Gentle said they had to fill their storehouses with acorns and other nuts before winter came. Once we even saw a rabbit.

Seeing all the animals reminded Christi of the conversation at supper the night before. "Do you think we'll see any deer today? I'd like to pet one. I did that once at a petting zoo."

"It's possible that we could see some at a distance," answered Mr. Friendson, "but I am sure we are making too much noise for them to be close. Deer in the wild are a lot different from deer raised in a petting zoo. Here, man is their enemy, not their friend."

We continued to tromp along, captivated with all the new sights and sounds and smells of the forest. Maybe that's why most of us completely forgot about collecting things for the scavenger hunt.

One of us did remember though. "Here's a red leaf," said Hapford, unexpectedly bending over to scoop it up.

Ronny, like me, was taking in all the fascinating things of the forest and not watching ahead. Hapford's unexpected stop caught him off guard, and he tripped right over Hapford, who was in a very awkward position with his head down. They both ended up sprawling in the wet leaves.

Immediately Ronny accused angrily, "Why did you stop like that?" He balled up one fist and tackled poor Hapford.

Reginald and I grabbed at Ronny's jacket and pulled him off. He was about ready to sock me too, so I had to do some quick thinking.

"Ronny, you can't hit me! I'm your buddy," I said in a loud voice.

It worked. He dropped his fist and started brushing himself off, muttering under his breath. The ruckus had gotten the attention of both Pastor Gentle and Mr. Thriftmore. They dutifully inspected both boys to see that they were okay.

It gave us all an opportunity to catch our breath, and since fall leaves were everywhere, other buddies began collecting too. That's when I realized it was happening again. Buddies were working together and feeling special loyalty to one another—even Ronny and I. It was a good opportunity to bring up what had been bothering me since breakfast.

"Ronny, do you remember last night and how scared you were?" I asked.

He stiffened and lowered his eyebrows. "I wasn't scared. You were the scaredy-cat," he denied.

"But I heard you pray," I protested.

"You were dreaming. That's all. Why would I want to talk with Pastor Gentle?"

Whoops! He had let it out. I hadn't been dreaming. "You really do need the Lord," I said. "We're buddies, and I want you to know Jesus."

"If you are my buddy, leave me alone."

I didn't say any more about his prayer, and we continued picking up leaves until we found the ones that suited us—you know, bright in color and perfectly shaped. We even found some acorns.

Not far away the stranger was watching—unbeknownst to us. Voices carry very well in the forest, and he could hear what Ronny had said.

"What a foolish young man," he whispered; and, thinking of his own youth, sadness clouded his eyes. Watching us and listening to our conversations, the flood of memories continued coming. How he wished he could go back and change the wasted fourteen years.

"Since we've stopped," said Mr. Friendson, "let's have a little science lesson. Do you know why leaves turn colors?"

"Because it's fall," answered J. Michael confidently.

"Well, that's **when** they change, but that's not **why** they change," said Mr. Friendson.

"Doesn't it have something to do with having a frost?" suggested Ace.

"That has something to do with it."

Reginald was about to burst with the answer, but he gave the others a chance first. Finally, he had to speak up. "A drop in temperature induces the breakdown of chlorophyll in deciduous broad leaves. This permits the underlying xanthophyll or carotene pigment to appear. Chilling temperatures, along with shortened daylight hours, also disrupt photosynthesis and prompt the leaves to wither."

"So what does that mean?" asked Ronny. He was as much in the dark as I was.

Racer spoke up. "Doesn't it just mean that when the days grow shorter and the temperature drops, the cold ruins the green color that is in leaves? Other colors that were hidden all the time begin to show up."

"That's very simply put," agreed Mr. Friendson, "but also fairly accurate."

Behind a tree not far away—we found out later— our spy could hardly keep from laughing out loud. It was the first time he had felt anything close to happiness in a long time. He wanted to run out and say, "Mr. Friendson, I know why you know so much about all this. We both heard about the trees and animals when we were boys and went on hikes at Camp Friendship. I know where you are headed today. I've already been there and had my breakfast."

Not Mr. Friendson, not Pastor Gentle, not any of us knew we had company on this hike; but it was time to move on. The trail began to lead along a high, sharp ridge. We were also heading west, according to Ronny. The sun was a lot higher in the sky now and shining through the trees. Banks of fluffy clouds could be seen in the distance. In places, we could see out over the valley. Mr. Friendson didn't stop to let us climb out on any of the rocks. Was I ever glad of that!

Tramp, tramp. Things were starting to get pretty monotonous . . . when up ahead Racer darted off like a scared rabbit into the underbrush.

"Where are you going?" yelled Booker, his buddy. "Wait for me."

"I see an empty bird's nest," Racer called back. "Come and help me get it."

The rest of us looked but didn't see the bird's nest, at least not at first. It was well hidden. Besides, there would only be one. Why should the rest of us take the chance of finding a snake or even a bear? Mr. Friendson quickly followed the boys to see that they didn't get into a dangerous situation. The underbrush was so thick that we really could not see what was going on. Suddenly we heard Mr. Friendson's voice. "No, no! Leave it alone! That's not a bird's nest. It's a hornets' nest!"

"Hornets!" screamed a voice that sounded very much like Racer's. Next, we heard thrashing and crashing. "Yeow!"

The thrashing and crashing continued. It sounded like Booker and Racer were fighting something or trying to escape.

"A-a-augh!!!" That was Booker. "It has me by the hair!"

On the trail, the rest of us stood still with our eyes big and our mouths open. We expected to see swarming hornets or something worse come bounding out at us any time.

"Stand still!" shouted Mr. Friendson, still hidden in the underbrush. The crashing and thrashing finally stopped. In a few moments, he came out grasping two red-faced boys. There were rips in their clothes and scratches on their faces and hands. They had gone after a hornets' nest all right, but, thankfully, it was an empty one. The real monster was the brambles. When Booker and Racer started thrashing around to get away from the hornets they thought were there, they ran into brambles. The more they tried to get out, the more they got caught and scratched. The woods is no place to lose your head.

Pastor Gentle pulled the first-aid kit out of one of his big pockets and handed it to Mr. Friendson. Racer and Booker flinched a little as he began cleaning their scratches and rubbing on first-aid cream.

"You'll be good as new by the time we get back," said Pastor Gentle encouragingly. "Those brambles put up quite a fight, didn't they?" He chuckled a little.

The boys were smiling and seemed "not much the worse for wear" as Pastor Gentle put it.

There was just one thing. "Booker, please forgive me for getting you into such a mess," said Racer in an apologetic tone. "If you hadn't followed me, you wouldn't have gotten all scratched up. Look, you even tore your jacket."

"Oh, I'll heal," said Booker bravely, now that the real scare was over. "I forgive you, and I think Mom can patch my jacket. Every time I see the patch, I will remember that we are buddies. It's almost as good as having a brother, wouldn't you say?"

We were soon on our way again. The sun was really getting high, and I was hot from all the hiking . . . and hungry.

"How soon do we stop to eat?" I called to Mr. Friendson.

"It's not far now," he called back over his shoulder.

Had we gone a few yards into the woods, past that bramble patch, instead of on down the forest path, we would have come upon a sad scene. Someone who knew these woods better than any of us sat on a rock with his head in his hands. He had heard Racer ask for forgiveness, and he had heard Dooker say "I forgive you." That's what he wanted too—forgiveness. But was forgiveness possible? Not only did he need to ask God to forgive him, there were other people he had hurt. He needed to ask their forgiveness too. But that would be so hard. He sat and thought for a long while. Finally, he decided not to follow us any more. With deep sadness, he headed in the opposite direction.

CHAPTER 14

HOBO STEW

It took about fifteen more minutes to hike to the place where we were having our cookout; and, gratefully, it was nearly all downhill. The trail veered south from the high ridge and wound down into a wide canyon. We knew it was south because Ronny, of course, pulled out his compass to remind us. I was thinking more highly of that compass too. It might be nice to have one of my own. The sun was shining almost overhead, and my stomach was growling. Before long, most of us had taken off our jackets and tied them around our waists.

In some places the trail was pretty steep and our feet slid on loose stones. The challenge of getting down the steep trail safely made us feel more like real hikers, and it kept us on our toes also. It was a great idea to have a buddy. At times all of us needed help, and buddies could hold on to each other.

"We're almost there," called Mr. Friendson from the front of our troop. "Is everyone doing okay?"

"Yes," most of us called back.

I did notice that Pastor Gentle was really leaning on his walking stick or fishing pole, whichever it was.

He used it to keep his balance and to test for loose stones. His face was flushed and covered with beads of perspiration. Obviously, hiking was not something he did every weekend.

"Why did you come on the retreat, Pastor Gentle?" asked J. Michael with some concern in his voice. He was right beside his pastor, but he couldn't have done much had Pastor Gentle slipped. "Maybe someone else should have come in your place."

"Don't worry, J. Michael," the pastor said, taking a quick gasp of air. "I'll be fine." He puffed and grunted some more. "I guess I forgot . . . *gasp* . . . how steep this hiking trail was. Whew!" He stopped, pulled off his hat, and wiped his sweating forehead. "I'm glad I came, though." He took a quick sip from his canteen, put his hat back on and started on down the trail. "This has brought back many memories, . . . *gasp* . . . and it has been good to see Aunt Ruth and Uncle Jake again. The only sad thing has been to see how the camp has fallen into disrepair. There is no way they will be able to continue this ministry unless someone helps them."

While Pastor Gentle was talking, I noticed some things around us had changed. The air was cooler;

and, faintly at first, then more clearly, I could hear rushing water.

The trail soon became level and wider. Finally, we were in a clearing under some huge pines. A small, clear mountain stream was gushing downhill over many rocks. No picture could have been more beautiful. God is a wonderful Artist and Creator.

"Oh, this is gorgeous," gasped Miss Content, catching her breath. "It's perfect for our cookout. What do you want us to do to help, Mr. Friendson?"

"Nothing just yet," he said. "Take a rest. I'll let you know when we're ready to work."

Most of us sprawled on the heavy blanket of pine needles that covered the area. Then it hit me.

"Needle," I whispered to Ronny. "That's one of the things on our list. Mr. Friendson didn't say what kind of needle. Maybe the rest won't think of it."

"Yeah," snickered Ronny. He liked my bright idea, and he slyly picked up several long pine needles and tucked them into his backpack.

I noticed that Booker and Racer were smearing more first-aid cream on each other. Susie was checking to see if her "pets" were enjoying the trip. She even got Miriam to pick one up and put it on a rock in the sun. Immediately it changed to the color

of the rock. Hapford and Reginald were checking out the area with list in hand. I was sure they had collected more items than any of us. I wondered if they had found a "needle" yet. Sandy and Christi were hunkered down at the edge of the mountain stream. They were splashing their hands in the cold water. I found out later that they were collecting pretty stones. Ace and J. Michael were helping Mr. Friendson and Mr. Thriftmore unload their backpacks. Pastor Gentle was resting against one of the tall pines, catching his breath and flapping his hat in front of his face like a fan. He said there were some mountain trout in the stream; but, since he didn't have his fishing line and hooks, we wouldn't have fish for lunch.

Finally, *Twe-e-et!!!* There was the whistle.

"Ready for hobo stew?" Mr. Friendson asked, rubbing his hands together in anticipation.

"Yes!"

"Are we ever!"

"Bring it on!"

"Whoa, not so fast," he said. "The thing that makes hobo stew so good is that everyone helps make it. See that circle of rocks? We need wood to build a fire there."

J. Michael and Ace volunteered to go gather some wood and build the fire. They were surprised to find that the rocks were still warm. Someone had recently had a fire there. Mr. Friendson had no explanation at the time, but you've figured it out, haven't you?

Mr. Friendson looked around. "Racer, do you still have your Super Sport?"

"Yes, sir," Racer answered enthusiastically, holding it up.

"Good. Here are four cans of tomatoes. You have a can opener, so we will let you and Booker open the tomatoes. Deal?"

"Deal!" agreed Racer. He had been waiting for a reason to use his Super Sport again.

"I need more volunteers," said Mr. Friendson. "Here are a bag of potatoes and some paring knives. Who wants the job?"

"We'll do it!" shouted Susie, shooting up her hand. That should certainly guarantee that she would not have to do dishes.

"And I'll help them," announced Miss Content. It did seem like a pretty big job.

Susie scooped up her "pets," and Miss Content got the bag of potatoes and the paring knives. I really hoped no lizards would end up in the stew.

"Now, who will clean the carrots?" Mr. Friendson held up two bunches that looked like they had just been pulled out of the ground. I was all ready to volunteer, but Ronny looked at me as if to say, "Wait. Maybe we won't have to do anything."

It didn't matter because Sandy and Christi volunteered. It seemed they would do just about anything to get to play in the water.

Mr. Friendson began looking around for other volunteers. "Oh, yes, I almost forgot. It is a tearful job, but who will peel and chop up some onions?" he asked half apologetically. "Hapford and Reginald, how about you?"

"Yes, sir," they answered with less than the usual enthusiasm, but then Reginald remembered his chemistry. "If we wash them in the cold stream first, they won't make our eyes water so much," he said encouragingly to Hapford.

Everyone seemed to have such great team spirit that I felt bad. Ronny and I had not volunteered for any job. If Mr. Friendson followed the Scriptural principle—and I was sure he would—Ronny and I might not get anything to eat.

He hadn't forgotten us, though. "That leaves you, Ronny and Pudge. You will be our cooks. Here is what you will need." He handed us a package of ground meat, a long, clean stick, and a very large, empty tin can.

"How can we cook in a tin can?" questioned Ronny.

I was a little puzzled too. "What is the stick for?" I asked.

"We're making hobo stew, remember?" said Mr. Friendson. "We're going to cook like hobos. The tin can is your pot, and the stick is for stirring."

Pastor Gentle began to chuckle. "Necessity is the mother of invention. Ask any hobo."

We all looked at each other and began to laugh too. So this was hobo stew. We were going to cook and eat out of a tin can! I wondered what this stew would taste like.

If the stranger in the woods had been there, he could have told us that he had eaten hobo stew many times—and not always in such a pretty setting. Hopping trains and living in a hobo jungle among others who did the same, he nearly always cooked over an open fire and had often eaten out of a can that wasn't as clean as ours. He hadn't always had such good things to put into his stew either, but he wasn't there, and what he faced was not going to be easy. However, we didn't know anything about that just yet.

About forty-five minutes later, when the coals were hot, everyone added their contribution to the "pot." When our meal had simmered for just the right amount of time, Mr. Friendson dipped it up. It was the best stew I had ever eaten—maybe because I was so hungry and maybe because all my friends had helped fix it. Mr. Friendson had also brought along the leftover biscuits from breakfast. They were just as good as ever, and, thankfully, no lizard ended up in the pot—at least not that I knew of!

CHAPTER 15

BUDDIES TO THE RESCUE

We took care of cleanup in no time. Although we cooked like hobos, we ate in a more customary way—with disposable bowls and spoons—except for Racer's Super Sport spoon. There were no leftovers. Every single drop of hobo stew and every crumb of breakfast biscuit were gobbled up. We weren't overstuffed, but we were satisfied.

While Mr. Thriftmore and Mr. Friendson took care of the trash, put water on the fire, scattered the coals, and loaded their backpacks again, we had one last chance to explore the lovely campsite.

Everyone was hoping to find more items from the scavenger list. Racer and Booker had given up hunting for a bird's nest. Instead, they had spotted some birch trees off to the right. Racer was using his Super Sport to hack white bark from a branch that had fallen to the ground. They already had an empty eggshell.

Ronny and I were nearby. We hadn't found either a bird's nest or an empty eggshell, and we needed a piece of white birch bark also. The only things we did have were the red and yellow leaves, a pine cone, and the acorns we had found at the very beginning of the hike. Of course, we did have our needles.

Reginald and Hapford were searching the stream bank. They found a white stone and thought they might also find a needle that someone had dropped there.

Ace and J. Michael said they had collected nearly everything from the list. Their only problem was to decide how they would carry back the fuzzy caterpillar they had found—and who would carry it.

The girls were playing at the stream. They wanted to splash their toes in the water. Miss Content reminded them that, although the sun was shining brightly, the mountain water was cold. The girls were persuasive, and finally she agreed to let them see for themselves. They soon found she was right and had already put their socks back on.

While they did, Susie decided to give her "pets" one last time in the sun. Although Miriam had accepted the "pets," Christi and Sandy were not so sure, and they certainly did not want one to crawl into their shoes.

"Please put your lizards back in your pocket," Christi said in a pleading but nonthreatening tone. "I know they are your 'pets,' but they make my skin prickly."

Well, that was the wrong thing to say to Susie. "My 'pets' won't hurt you," she said, giving Christi a little shove. "You better get used to them, because I'm taking them home with me."

It was not a big shove, but it was enough to push Christi off balance, especially since she was sitting right on the edge of the stream bank. She flailed her arms and tried to get her balance by turning the way she was falling. It almost worked. She caught her balance without actually falling into the water and getting completely soaked. However, her stocking feet did end up where she didn't want them—back in the icy water.

"Help!" she cried. We all ran in that direction. It sounded like she needed help. It was just the coldness of the water that had caused her startled cry, but she wasn't hurt.

When Ronny caught up with me, all he could say was "I don't see what the big deal is."

There was one small problem, though. Remember, before Susie pushed her off balance, Christi had already put her socks back on. Thankfully, her shoes were dry, but her feet, along with her socks, were really wet. She held her socks up and wrung them out to show everyone.

"Look what you've done to my buddy!" shrieked Sandy with her hands on her hips and her contorted face close to Susie's.

Miss Content came running. "Are you all right, Christi?" she asked first. Then turning to Susie, she said softly, "Why did you push Christi?"

"She deserved it! She doesn't like my 'pets.' I guess I showed her."

"Oh, Susie," said Miriam sadly. "We are all friends. Now Christi has no dry socks to wear home. Aren't you sorry for what you did?"

"No," said Susie sharply. "If she had left my 'pets' alone, she wouldn't have wet socks." She turned away in a huff.

Poor Susie. She really didn't know anything about heartfelt repentance. She simply justified her actions, thinking that made them okay.

Sandy, on the other hand, felt guilty. It was wrong to yell at Susie. As Pastor Gentle would have said, "Two wrongs don't make a right."

Calmly she said honestly and directly to Susie, "Please forgive me. I should not have yelled at you."

"Forget it," snarled Susie. She walked away guarding her "pets," which were now safely tucked away in her jacket pocket.

From a distance, the rest of us watched the goings-on with open mouths, but we said nothing.

Like everyone who had followed Mr. Friendson's advice, Sandy had on two pairs of socks. Even though she might get a blister on the way back to Camp Friendship, she pulled off one pair and insisted that Christi wear them. "We're buddies and friends," she said. "I know you would do the same for me."

Again something special was happening. Buddies were helping each other.

Then, all too soon, we heard, *Twe-e-et!!!*

"Time to head back," called Mr. Friendson. "Everybody ready?"

There were a few groans, but Mr. Friendson ignored them.

"If we keep moving, we should get back to Camp Friendship in less than two hours," he said.

It had been an adventure and almost fun to follow the trail down to the campsite, but now we had to climb the path back up the ridge. That was not going to be so easy. As we started out, Mr. Friendson called out, "Hang on to your gear."

I saw Ronny pat his pocket to make sure the compass was there. He smiled a satisfied smile.

Then Racer unexpectedly shouted, "Mr. Friendson, I don't have my Super Sport! I must have left it over by the birch tree. Please wait while I go get it." He started running in that direction with Mr. Friendson tagging along behind.

"How many delays are we going to have?" growled Ronny under his breath. "First the girls, now Racer." He was impatient to get going.

The rest of us waited and watched as Mr. Friendson and Racer looked for the Super Sport. They looked and looked, retracing Racer's steps from the birch tree to the campfire site and back several times. Mr. Friendson even looked in Racer's backpack and in the stream. There was no Super Sport.

"It has to be here," said Racer desperately.

We all went back and helped look. The Super Sport was nowhere to be found. We even looked through the trash.

"Could a raccoon have confiscated it?" asked Reginald. He was always looking for a logical explanation.

"I suppose that is possible," said Mr. Friendson, half chuckling, "but it is highly unlikely."

There was really no better explanation though, and the sun was moving farther west all the time. At last Mr. Friendson said, "I'm very sorry, Racer, but we have to go. We'll report it when we get back, and maybe another group will find it later."

"How will I explain my carelessness to Dad when I get home?" Racer groaned. "This has ruined the whole retreat for me."

It had put a definite blotch on an otherwise pleasant hike, yet there seemed nothing else to do. We had to head back to Camp Friendship.

Spirits and tempers were not in great shape as we scratched and scrambled our way up the trail to the ridge. About fifteen minutes later, Mr. Friendson called breathlessly from the narrow trail up ahead. "We're almost . . . to the ridge."

That was just about when some stones came rolling down the trail toward Ronny and me and Mr. Thriftmore. What was happening? We couldn't see.

"A-a-augh!" J. Michael let out a terrible yell, and more gravel and stones went flying by.

"You're okay," I heard Pastor Gentle say. "Here, grab my walking stick." Since we couldn't see, all we could do was listen and speculate as to what was happening.

"O-ow, o-ow! I think I twisted my ankle!" cried J. Michael.

Somehow Mr. Friendson and Pastor Gentle managed to get J. Michael to the level ground of the ridge, where Mr. Friendson examined the ankle more closely. He finally determined it wasn't broken but had been twisted. It hurt and was tender to the touch.

"If you had a crutch to lean on, or even a walking stick like Pastor Gentle's, you wouldn't have to put so much weight on your ankle until we get back to the camp," said Mr. Friendson.

Of course, Pastor Gentle quickly offered, "You may use my walking stick, son."

"Pastor!" spoke up Ace. "You need that walking stick. J. Michael can lean on me. He's my buddy. I'll help him back to Camp Friendship." He grabbed J. Michael's arm and draped it over his own shoulder.

By the time we got back to Camp Friendship two hours later, we must have looked like soldiers returning from battle. Racer and Booker had red scratches on their arms and faces as well as torn clothes. Pastor Gentle was leaning heavily on his walking cane. J. Michael and Ace were clinging to each other—J. Michael hopping on one foot at times.

Sandy and Christi were walking like their feet were sore, and all of us were dirty and very rumpled.

Our spirits were at the lowest they'd been in the last two days, and we were totally unprepared for what awaited us back at the camp.

It seemed that when the spy who had been watching us left us in the woods, he had gone back to Camp Friendship. As we came up to the Camp Office, we certainly were not expecting the puzzling scene. On the front porch were Aunt Ruth, Uncle Jake, and a man we'd not seen the whole time we'd been at the camp. What was he doing here? Why hadn't we seen him before? Was there a problem? What was his connection with Aunt Ruth and Uncle Jake?

The stranger was tall and slightly stooped, and he looked to be about Mr. Friendson's age. He wasn't exactly what you'd call scroungy. In fact, he looked like he had just gotten out of the shower because his hair was still wet and his face was ruddy as if he had just shaved. His hair was gray and long, though neatly combed back over his ears—like he knew it needed to be cut, but for some reason had not had it done. Both Aunt Ruth and Uncle Jake evidently knew him. To our utter amazement, they were hugging him, and he was hugging them back! There certainly didn't seem to be a problem. Instead they all seemed overjoyed. We were confused. Who was this visitor? Why did Aunt Ruth and Uncle Jake seem so excited? We'd never seen them so animated.

We continued to watch in total amazement. Then suddenly Pastor Gentle gasped and put his hand to his chest. I thought he must be having a heart attack because of exhaustion from the hike. "Oh, my!" he cried. "Can it be?"

Mr. Friendson's mouth dropped open. I have never seen him look so speechless. His hands dropped to his sides; his face went pale. He let out what sounded like a groan; then he started toward the porch. "David? My old buddy, David?" he asked hopefully—weakly.

Pastor Gentle finally recovered but all he could say was, "It's a miracle!"

Mr. Friendson and Pastor Gentle pushed ahead of us. You've figured it out too, haven't you? It dawned on the rest of us more slowly. The stranger was David, the prodigal son of Aunt Ruth and Uncle Jake. For fourteen years he had been living as a hobo—riding the rails, sleeping in boxcars, traveling and working from town to town, seeing the country.

There was a lot more to his story, and we soon heard it all.

CHAPTER 16

GOOD-BYE TO NEW FRIENDS

The next two hours went by in a flash. Although Mr. Friendson and Pastor Gentle wanted to hear David's story, they gave us their attention first.

"Rest for a few minutes while I go inside and see if the cook is ready for us," said Mr. Friendson. "I asked him to have a little treat ready when we got back."

What I wouldn't have given for another bowl of hobo stew just then. I would even have eaten some leftover oatmeal.

When the dinner bell rang, it sounded so-o good, and we crowded through the door. There, on a table near the blazing fireplace, were big mugs, pitchers of steaming hot cocoa, and plates stacked high with giant cookies—raisin oatmeal, peanut butter, and old-fashioned ginger. Pastor Gentle said grace and thanked the Lord for safety on the hike, and for the miracle of David's safe return. He also asked that Racer's Super Sport would be found. Then we dug in. You have never seen cookies and hot cocoa disappear so fast.

While we refueled, Aunt Ruth, Uncle Jake, and their restored and forgiven prodigal son David joined us.

Mr. Friendson and Pastor Gentle asked most of the questions. "Where have you been? Why didn't you let someone know where you were? Are you back to stay?"

It was just as Mr. Friendson had said during devotions that morning. David had received Christ as his Saviour as a boy, but when God spoke to him as a young man about total surrender to God's will, he refused to listen and ran away. For fourteen years, he had been running from God, but he had never run beyond God's loving call. He couldn't get away from God's conviction in his rebellious heart. He also couldn't get away from the prayers of his camp buddy, and especially the prayers of his father and mother, Uncle Jake and Aunt Ruth.

"So, what is God leading you to do now, David?" asked Pastor Gentle.

"I'm home where I belong, and I want Camp Friendship to be my ministry as well as Dad and Mom's.

"God works in marvelous ways. A train finally brought me this way, and I had to see what had happened while I was gone. When I stopped, I never intended to stay or let anyone know I was here. It was just another stop on my hobo journey. I spent one night in David's Hideaway. That hasn't changed much." He chuckled, and we knew what he meant.

David continued. "The next afternoon the Highland bus rolled up with my old buddy from summer camp days. You haven't changed much, buddy," he said, grinning at Mr. Friendson and giving him a friendly slap on the shoulder. "Then, when Pastor Gentle got out, I couldn't believe it. All my recollections of the old days came back, but fourteen years make a big difference. Back then, we didn't seem so different; now you both have a purpose in life. I don't. Look at us. I have nothing, and you both have a rich ministry to young people. It is you who have found real happiness and success."

When he said that, I noticed tears well up in both Pastor Gentle's and Mr. Friendson's eyes. No doubt about it, we are important to them. It makes me want to serve the Lord even more.

While we continued munching cookies and sipping hot chocolate, Uncle Jake said, "Tell them the rest, son."

"Well, of course, I needed something to eat these last few days, so I scavenged food out of the kitchen. I have asked my parents to forgive me for that. Pastor Gentle, please forgive me for using your fishing line and hooks without permission also.

"You know, buddy," he said, grinning again at Mr. Friendson, "when you put that new lock on the kitchen, I had quite a time getting in."

Mr. Friendson laughed loudly and slapped his knees at the thought of how his concerned repair had thwarted David's crime. It was a relief to know no dangerous criminal had broken in.

"Go on," invited Pastor Gentle. He was as anxious as we were to find out what else God had done in David's heart.

"Well, I've been watching these young people." He gestured toward the tables where we were stuffing ourselves with cookies and hot chocolate. "You didn't know I was watching you, of course, but your Godly character and actions really made me stop and look at my own life."

He turned again to Pastor Gentle and Mr. Friendson. "These young people need a place like Camp Friendship. There is plenty of work to be done around here, and I'm staying if Dad and Mom will have me." He looked at Uncle Jake and Aunt Ruth. A plea reflected from his eyes.

"Have you?" declared Aunt Ruth in a broken voice. "Oh, son, you are an answer to years of prayer. As Pastor Gentle prayed, it is a miracle. Of course we want you here—if that is what God wants, and surely it is."

Uncle Jake added without hesitation, "All is forgiven, son. This is your ministry now. As Mother said, it is an answer to our prayers. We want you here. There is so much to do that I 'can't shake a stick at it,' as Pastor Gentle would say. You can even fix up our old log cabin, and then we can move back in."

"Oh, wouldn't that be wonderful!" gasped Aunt Ruth, clasping her hands in front of her face. Tears squeezed out the corners of her eyes.

We could have sat all day and listened to David tell of his life and adventures and hardships as a hobo, but our time at Camp Friendship was almost over. As Pastor Alltruth had predicted, it was a memorable experience in more ways than one. I learned more about what it means to be, as well as to have, a friend. I learned how important Godly character and actions are, but most important, I learned a valuable lesson about God's will and about God's patient working in our lives.

Before we left, Mr. Friendson announced that Reginald and Hapford had won the scavenger hunt, and he presented them with a rustic-looking pine plaque. Burned into the plaque in crude lettering was "Good Woodsmen's Award."

"I think we should have gotten an award too," complained Ronny. "After all, with my compass we kept everyone from getting lost." I remembered our squirrel-chasing adventure and raised one eyebrow at him.

Now the only unsolved problem was Racer's lost Super Sport. When David heard about it, he said, "I'm sure it must be there at the campsite. Things can hide in the pine needles and grass. I'll go there tomorrow and look around. I feel certain I can find it. You pray for me, Racer, that God will help me. Okay?"

"I will pray very hard," assured Racer.

I was already starting to like David. *What a good buddy he must have been,* I thought.

"I'm going to bring the bus around now," announced Mr. Friendson. "Run to your lodges and get your sleeping bags and luggage. Be back here with everything in ten minutes. Girls, I'll be up to Queen Esther's Lodge in a short while to help you carry your things."

When we got back to David's Hideaway Lodge, we weren't surprised to see Pastor Gentle's fishing line and hooks hanging on the nail beside the door.

Inside, only a few coals remained in the old potbellied stove. The same old, rusty beds were there, and the room was nearly as bare and drab as before, yet somehow it felt like home—not home-home, but home-away-from-home. I decided it was not the surroundings that made me feel that way. Having my friends nearby was what made me feel warm and at home. Although I love my friends, I was also anxious to be home. I couldn't even imagine how much David, the hobo prodigal, had missed home while he was running from God.

One last time we passed the washroom, and one last time we came to the fork in the path. The distance to the lodges had seemed so far the first time, but now it seemed short. The girls were coming, struggling with all their luggage. Mr. Friendson was helping them, and David had pitched in too.

Miriam was pleading. "Mr. Friendson, may Susie please take her 'pets' home? I will make sure she keeps them in her pocket."

Christi had something to say about that. "Mr. Friendson, please don't let her bring them."

"They will get loose for sure," continued Sandy.

"Please," begged Susie.

Mr. Friendson said, "I have an idea." He patted Susie on the head and strode off to the Camp Office. In a few minutes he was back with a quart-sized glass jar with holes in the lid.

"You may take your 'pets' home, Susie, if you will put them in this jar and let Miss Content keep them with her while we're on the bus."

Finally, the bus was loaded, and Mr. Friendson had just one last instruction. "If you enjoyed your time at Camp Friendship, go tell Aunt Ruth and Uncle Jake. But keep it short and get right onto the bus. You can see storm clouds piling up." He pointed toward the sky over the Camp Office. "I believe the weather Reginald was predicting is headed our way. I'd like to be down the mountain before it gets here."

When we said thank you, Aunt Ruth quietly said, "It is so wonderful" and dabbed some more at her eyes. She was talking about David's return as well as our visit, I'm sure.

Uncle Jake nodded to let us know he agreed. "Young people are always welcome here," he said.

It made me happy to see Aunt Ruth and Uncle Jake so happy.

"I will find that Super Sport for you, Racer," called David to a very grateful Racer, who was feeling better already.

Then Mr. Friendson blew his whistle one more time. "Come on," he said. "We must get started down the mountain."

I thought I felt a few raindrops as we ran to the bus and got on. Everyone took the same seats as before, except Mr. Thriftmore. He sat behind Mr. Friendson, I guess to keep him awake. Susie handed her jar of "pets" to Miss Content, and Ronny stashed his backpack up in the overhead rack as before. We flopped into our seats as Mr. Friendson cranked up the bus and pulled out. Waving from the windows, we could see that David had one arm around Aunt Ruth and the other around Uncle Jake. *What a miracle of God's grace, love, and forgiveness,* I thought.

We were barely back onto the winding mountain road when I saw that Pastor Gentle was sound asleep with his head resting against the window—no games on the trip home. It was just sprinkling, but we all saw the dark sky and heard a distant rumble. A storm was coming for sure. Mr. Friendson turned the windshield wipers on slow speed. The tapping

rhythm had its effect. Soon Booker and Racer, J. Michael and Ace, and Sandy and Christi were bunking up in their seats. Miriam and Susie were talking quietly. Only Reginald and Hapford were looking out the windows.

"I don't know about you," I said to Ronny, "but I'm going to take a nap as soon as we are down this mountain." I remembered the road and wanted to make sure Mr. Friendson got us safely to the bottom. I saw the signs for **Falling Rocks** and **Mud Slides** again. *I sure hope it doesn't start raining hard while we're on this road,* I thought.

That was the last thing I remembered for quite a while. When I woke up again, it was raining hard, and the windshield wipers were flipping back and forth on high speed. Lightning zigzagged down from the sky all around us, and thunder rumbled loudly. Since it was so dark outside, I figured it must be somewhere around six o'clock. We had made it down the mountain safely and were on our way home, but we weren't there yet.

CHAPTER 17

A STARTLING DISCOVERY

The thunder and lightning woke a few others, including Pastor Gentle. He yawned, rubbed his hand across his eyes, and looked out the window. Then he called softly so he wouldn't disturb anyone who was still sleeping.

"Where are we, Mr. Thriftmore?"

"We're about fifteen minutes out of Harmony," Mr. Thriftmore responded quietly.

They kept talking in low voices. They didn't know the storm had wakened some of the rest of us.

"How long has it been raining?" Pastor Gentle asked.

"It started raining before we were all the way down the mountain, but not nearly this hard. The thunder and lightning really started about five minutes ago. I think we must be driving right into the storm. I'm trying to help Mr. Friendson watch the road. It's hard to see."

"Is there anything I can do?"

"Just keep the children occupied if they wake up," interjected Mr. Friendson. "We don't want them to be frightened—and please pray."

We rode along quietly for another ten minutes.

Suddenly the bus bounced with a hard jolt. *A big pothole,* I thought immediately.

BOOM! . . . PLOP! BUMP! PLOP! BUMP!

Everyone immediately awoke with a start.

"What did we hit?"

"What was that?"

Mr. Friendson slowed the bus and eased it to the side of the road.

"Everyone stay calm," said Pastor Gentle. He kept saying everything would be okay—that Mr. Friendson and Mr. Thriftmore would take care of the problem.

At the front of the bus, our drill sergeant and Booker's dad were hunting for an umbrella or raincoat. They finally found an umbrella.

"It must be a flat tire," said Mr. Thriftmore. "I just hope hitting that pothole didn't break anything else. If I may have the umbrella, I'll go take a look."

Rain was still pouring down "in bucketfuls" as Pastor Gentle said. Mr. Thriftmore got out, went around the back of the bus to check, and was back quickly. The umbrella had helped, but he was still wet, especially his feet. He shook off the umbrella and brushed at his clothes.

"It's a flat tire all right. Looks like a blowout. It's a good thing it is on the back where we have dual wheels. One tire is ruined, but nothing else is broken that I can see."

With Mr. Thriftmore up front, Mr. Friendson moved back to where we were. He gave us an encouraging smile. "You have all been brave campers on this trip. I am very pleased. We've had some challenges, and now we have another one, but the Lord will take care of us this time too. He watched over David all those years and brought him home safely. You can be certain He knows about our problem."

He really made us feel much better. He even said we were brave. Our spirits perked up.

"Now, let's ask the Lord to direct us again. He has a purpose in all this." Turning to Pastor Gentle, he said, "Pastor, will you ask God for His wisdom?"

Pastor Gentle nodded and began praying. There was no doubt that he and the Lord had talked often before. When he said "Amen," I believe we all felt better—all except Ronny and Susie. They were never comfortable when we prayed or talked about God's watchful care over us.

"I have a suggestion," said Mr. Thriftmore. "I know there is a garage about a mile down the road.

We can drive slowly and get there. One tire is ruined, but the other one on that side can get us to the garage. We can pull the bus inside there; then, we can call the parents to come and pick up the children and their luggage at the garage."

"That sounds like a wonderful idea," said Mr. Friendson.

I glanced outside. It looked like the rain had let up some, but it certainly had not stopped. Mr. Friendson climbed into the driver's seat again and started the bus. Slowly he pulled back onto the highway. Praise the Lord, there was not much traffic. The tire continued its Plop! Bump! Plop! Bump! but in less than five minutes, we were at the garage. Just as Mr. Thriftmore said, we were able to pull the bus inside.

The garage manager took one look at the tire and agreed with Mr. Thriftmore's suggestion to call for rides. While he and Mr. Friendson did that, the rest of us got off the bus to stretch our legs. We all needed restroom breaks, but—wouldn't you know it— the restroom entrances were outside! I felt like we were back at Camp Friendship. Actually, it was a good feeling. Pastor Gentle and Miss Content supervised the use of the umbrella for the trips back and forth. Before we knew it, Mrs. Gentle, Mr. and Mrs. Peace, the Kindharts, and Mrs. Thriftmore arrived from Harmony.

We were very glad to see them. Pastor Gentle gave his wife a big hug, and she gently patted his cheeks and asked, "Are you and the children all right, dear?" She looked him up and down until she was satisfied he was "not much the worse for wear," as he would say.

When Racer and Booker said good-bye, Booker said, "Buddies stick together, and we have the scratches to prove it. Right?" For a moment, Racer forgot about his Super Sport, and they both laughed, remembering their tangle with the brambles. Then Booker added, "I am praying that your Super Sport will turn up, but if it doesn't, I know your father will be understanding. You are not a careless person."

"Thank you, Booker," said Racer. "You have been a great buddy, and we will always be friends."

Miriam seemed truly sorry that she had to say good-bye to Susie. Although Susie hadn't been the perfect buddy, Miriam still wanted to be her friend. "Take good care of those 'pets,'" she said, smiling. Then she gave Susie a hug. "God will take good care of you too, if you will let Him."

"Yeah, well, maybe," she said, shrugging.

Miriam certainly shows the genuine kindness and love of the Lord, I thought.

The Kindharts were a little disturbed to see J. Michael limping, but, as Ace helped him to the car, he said, "Now, if you ever need a crutch, just call me." They laughed and shook hands.

"It was great being your buddy," said J. Michael.

As the Kindharts drove away, Ace waved and called, "I will never forget this weekend. We will always be friends."

About that time, Mr. Virtueson drove up in the van from Highland Church. The rain had slowed, but there were still big water puddles and lots of mud. We couldn't help but get wet and muddy carrying our luggage out to the van. For some reason, I absent-mindedly said to Ronny, "I wonder which direction we go from here to get to Highland City?"

Once again, Ronny proudly reached into his pocket. "I can tell you." Then suddenly he had a ghastly look on his face. He dug his hand deeper into his pocket, then started slapping his hands over his other pockets. "Pudge, where is my compass?" he asked frantically. His eyes were bulging, and his cheeks had big red blotches.

"Isn't it in your pocket?" I asked. He had kept it there the whole weekend. Why wasn't it there now?

Anger began to show in his eyes. He had only one explanation. "Someone stole my compass!" he shouted. "Mr. Friendson, someone stole my compass!"

When Mr. Friendson heard the commotion, he came running. "What's the problem?"

"Someone stole my compass—the one my father gave me." If he hadn't been so angry, he probably would have cried.

"Calm down and we'll try to find it. Where did you have it last?"

"I had it on the bus. I know because I checked to see which way we were going to get home. I had it after we got here too . . . I think," he half screamed in exasperation.

"Maybe you dropped it on the bus. Let's go look." While the rest of us waited and watched from the van, Ronny and Mr. Friendson searched the bus; then they checked the restroom. I prayed they would find it. They looked all around the garage. They tried to retrace Ronny's steps everywhere he might have gone. He had been outside several times, and, with all the water, the compass could have easily been tramped into the mud if it had fallen out of his pocket.

"Could it be in your backpack?" asked Mr. Friendson.

"No!" answered Ronny emphatically. His "No" sounded more like "No, don't look in there" than "No, it is not in my backpack."

Mr. Friendson eyed him narrowly. "Let's just look," he said, as he started pulling it out of the van.

Ronny grabbed for his backpack, and something fell and clanked on the floor of the van.

"My Super Sport!" exclaimed Racer.

My mouth and everyone else's dropped open. You could have "knocked me over with a feather," as Pastor Gentle would have said.

Ronny hung his head and flung his backpack down in anger. Mr. Friendson picked up the Super Sport and handed it to Racer, who held it tightly to his chest. "Oh, thank You, Lord," he said, looking up as if he could actually see the Lord.

Ronny was furious. I don't know whether it was because he had been caught, or because he was angry at God for letting him lose his compass.

I suppose Mr. Friendson felt that "be sure your sin will find you out" had been illustrated quite well. He didn't say any more. He just sadly nodded to Mr. Virtueson as if to say, "We're ready to go home now."

It was very quiet on the ride back to Highland City. We all had much to think about. Mr. Friendson did tell Mr. Virtueson the exciting news about David and Aunt Ruth and Uncle Jake.

Ronny never said a word, though, and neither did I. When we finally got to his house, he looked at me with tight, white lips. "I guess this means we're not buddies any more, doesn't it?"

In a flash, all the things that had happened to us together that weekend went through my mind. Buddies stick by one another just as Booker had said. Ronny was not my buddy only when he did everything right. He was my buddy because I said I would be his buddy. That's what Camp Friendship was all about. "You're wrong, Ronny," I said quietly. "I was your buddy this weekend . . . and I will always be your friend. Just as Mr. Friendson prayed all those years for his buddy, I will keep praying for you, Ronny. You know God wants you to be His child."

"Don't talk to me about God. He doesn't care about me! If He did, why would He let me lose the compass that Dad gave me? I'm never going to let Him into my life!"

He slammed the door. It seemed we were no closer to seeing Ronny come to the Lord than we had ever been. But that doesn't stop me from continuing to pray for him.

Although I felt sad for Ronny, it really had been a wonderful retreat. I had learned many lessons.

Well, that's the story behind those muddy clothes hanging out of my hamper. Now I'm going to go to sleep. Good ni-i-ight.